Skye Fargo [...]
fight. But e[...]
from behind sent him reeling.

"I'll take you all on," Fargo growled at the circle of bruisers around him. "But one at a time. Not like a pack of wolves."

The men laughed and someone threw Slade a knife. Fargo knew the look in Slade's eyes. It was the look of a man who wouldn't be stopped until he or his opponent lay dead.

"Come on, guys, help me out," Slade spat, and Fargo was smashed down by a blow to the back. He felt Slade fall on top of him, crushingly, felt the cold bite of Slade's blade in his shoulder. Slade's knife poised just above Fargo's throat. It was all Fargo could do to keep it from descending.

His shoulder was cut bad, he knew. And it was the arm holding Slade's knife hand. He could feel the warm blood and deep throb of the wound, his strength running out, as slowly, slowly, Slade's knife came toward Fargo's throat.

The Trailsman lived by the code of the West. But now it looked like he was going to die by Yukon rules. . . .

**BE SURE TO READ
THE OTHER BOOKS IN THIS EXCITING
TRAILSMAN SERIES!**

① SIGNET

THE TRAILSMAN SERIES BY JON SHARPE

☐ THE TRAILSMAN #150: SAVAGE GUNS   (178866—$3.50)

☐ THE TRAILSMAN #151: CROW HEART'S REVENGE   (178874—$3.50)

☐ THE TRAILSMAN #152: PRAIRIE FIRE   (178882—$3.99)

☐ THE TRAILSMAN #153: SAGUARRO SHOWDOWN   (178890—$3.99)

☐ THE TRAILSMAN #154: AMBUSH AT SKULL PASS   (178904—$3.99)

☐ THE TRAILSMAN #155: OKLAHOMA ORDEAL   (178912—$3.99)

☐ THE TRAILSMAN #156: SAWDUST TRAIL   (181603—$3.99)

☐ THE TRAILSMAN #157: GHOST RANCH MASSACRE   (181611—$3.99)

☐ THE TRAILSMAN #158: TEXAS TERROR   (182154—$3.99)

☐ THE TRAILSMAN #159: NORTH COUNTRY GUNS   (182162—$3.99)

☐ THE TRAILSMAN #160: TORNADO TRAIL   (182170—$3.99)

*Prices slightly higher in Canada

Buy them at your local bookstore or use this convenient coupon for ordering.

PENGUIN USA
P.O. Box 999 — Dept. #17109
Bergenfield, New Jersey 07621

Please send me the books I have checked above.
I am enclosing $_____ (please add $2.00 to cover postage and handling). Send
check or money order (no cash or C.O.D.'s) or charge by Mastercard or VISA (with a $15.00
minimum). Prices and numbers are subject to change without notice.

Card #_____ Exp. Date _____
Signature_____
Name_____
Address_____
City _____ State _____ Zip Code _____

For faster service when ordering by credit card call **1-800-253-6476**

Allow a minimum of 4-6 weeks for delivery. This offer is subject to change without notice.

THE TRAILSMAN

163

YUKON MASSACRE

by

Jon Sharpe

A SIGNET BOOK

SIGNET
Published by the Penguin Group
Penguin Books USA Inc., 375 Hudson Street,
New York, New York 10014, U.S.A.
Penguin Books Ltd, 27 Wrights Lane,
London W8 5TZ, England
Penguin Books Australia Ltd, Ringwood,
Victoria, Australia
Penguin Books Canada Ltd, 10 Alcorn Avenue,
Toronto, Ontario, Canada M4V 3B2
Penguin Books (N.Z.) Ltd, 182–190 Wairau Road,
Auckland 10, New Zealand

Penguin Books Ltd, Registered Offices:
Harmondsworth, Middlesex, England

First published by Signet, an imprint of Dutton Signet,
a division of Penguin Books USA Inc.

First Printing, July, 1995
10 9 8 7 6 5 4 3 2 1

Copyright © Jon Sharpe, 1995
All rights reserved

The first chapter of this book appeared in *Revenge at Lost Creek*,
the one hundred sixty-second volume in this series.

 REGISTERED TRADEMARK—MARCA REGISTRADA

Printed in the United States of America

Without limiting the rights under copyright reserved above, no part of this
publication may be reproduced, stored in or introduced into a retrieval system,
or transmitted, in any form, or by any means (electronic, mechanical,
photocopying, recording, or otherwise), without the prior written permission of
both the copyright owner and the above publisher of this book.

BOOKS ARE AVAILABLE AT QUANTITY DISCOUNTS WHEN USED TO PROMOTE
PRODUCTS OR SERVICES. FOR INFORMATION PLEASE WRITE TO PREMIUM
MARKETING DIVISION, PENGUIN BOOKS USA INC., 375 HUDSON STREET, NEW
YORK, NEW YORK 10014.

If you purchased this book without a cover you should be aware that this book
is stolen property. It was reported as "unsold and destroyed" to the publisher
and neither the author nor the publisher has received any payment for this
"stripped book."

The Trailsman

Beginnings . . . they bend the tree and they mark the man. Skye Fargo was born when he was eighteen. Terror was his midwife, vengeance his first cry. Killing spawned Skye Fargo, ruthless, cold-blooded murder. Out of the acrid smoke of gunpowder still hanging in the air, he rose, cried out a promise never forgotten.

The Trailsman they began to call him all across the West: searcher, scout, hunter, the man who could see where others only looked, his skills for hire but not his soul, the man who lived each day to the fullest, yet trailed each tomorrow. Skye Fargo, the Trailsman, the seeker who could take the wildness of a land and the wanting of a woman and make them his own.

Russian America, 1860,
the vast and unforgiving land that will
become Alaska,
where the freezing cold makes every moment
a hunt for life
or a struggle against death . . .

1

Pete MacKenzie was right where they said he'd be—five miles east of the village of Alakanuk, at the bend of the creek. There the bitter wind howled through the yellow cedar and blasted off powdery snow from the surrounding hills. From far off echoed the call of a lone wolf. From nearby came the gurgle of water under the first coat of winter ice and the rhythmic squeak of the rawhide thong against the rough bark of a branch.

Suspended high above the fresh snow, MacKenzie's frozen corpse swung back and forth in the wind. His black hair was matted by snow, purplish face swollen almost beyond recognition. His hands hung heavy by his sides, the gloved fingers tipped with icicles.

The tall man stood for a long time, taking in the sight as the dim October light faded slowly. His lake blue eyes registered everything, the color of the dead man's flesh, the dark holes where four bullets had pierced the front of the moose-skin jacket, the tracks of frustrated wolves in the snow below. Death had been quick. And then MacKenzie's body had been hauled up high and left as some kind of warning. But a warning to whom?

Fargo swore under his breath. If only he'd got word from Pete sooner. Maybe he could have saved him. He cursed the senseless murder of a man as good as Pete MacKenzie. Cursed whoever did it. Cursed fate for keeping Pete's message from reaching him until it was too late. He glanced about him at the snow-covered bank and the dark forest that blanketed the hills, toward the banks of the Yukon River just a few miles away.

All around, the vastness of the northland seemed to press in on him and he heard again the call of wolves, the creak of the tall trees as they swayed in the wind. Night was coming, and winter was on the way. A helluva time to be up in Russian America, the wildest land on earth, a brutal place where only the brutal survived. He'd been up here once, a long time ago when he'd met up with Pete MacKenzie. And now he'd come back to find Pete dead.

Fargo drew his Colt and fired. The shot reverberated and a ptarmigan scuttled from beneath a nearby thicket. MacKenzie's body dropped onto the soft snow. Fargo drew his knife and cut the rawhide thong into pieces, then walked into the trees, his swallowtail snowshoes leaving a wide track in the fresh powder. He gathered several long branches and, using the rawhide, bent to the task of fashioning a travois. Fifteen minutes later, with MacKenzie's body strapped to the makeshift carrier, Fargo set off, hiking back toward the tiny fishing village of Alakanuk. Behind him, he dragged Pete MacKenzie's corpse.

MacKenzie had been one of the best trackers in the north. A silent man, a steady man, a man who could read the wind and move just as swiftly. He'd been a man who knew the ways of the north—where to set rabbit snares, find caribou herds and salmon. How to trap beaver, leaving the pregnant females so there'd be more the following year. How to keep warm in a blizzard. How to walk carefully, never making the one mistake that this unforgiving land could kill you for.

But MacKenzie had made a mistake, somewhere along the way. But it wasn't the land that had killed him. And Fargo knew he'd have to find whoever did it. It didn't matter that MacKenzie had been dead for at least a week and that the murderer could be hundreds of miles away by now. It didn't matter that winter was about to hit and the whole territory would soon be a frozen wasteland traveled only by wolves. Nothing mattered except finding the killer.

And as he tramped on through the darkening light, Fargo found himself thinking back to the night he got his last message from Pete MacKenzie. . . .

He'd found himself in Vancouver that night, at the Rusty Bullet Saloon with a buxom blonde named Sally on one knee and a straight flush spread out before him, facedown on the table. He was off two hundred dollars but winning this hand would put him well ahead for the night. He glanced into the cold eyes of the mustachioed gambling man sitting opposite him.

"Your bet, Mr. Fargo," the gambler said with a brief smile, his voice smooth as honey.

Sally flashed Fargo an encouraging smile and

fluffed her blond hair. Fargo's eyes narrowed a moment and he pretended to hesitate. His hand hovered over his remaining pile of silver and greenbacks and then he bent the edges of the cards upward as if convincing himself to lay a bet. With another glance toward the gambler, Fargo slowly pushed the remainder of his pile of silver and bills toward the center of the table.

"Wow," Sally said. She started to lean over to kiss him, but Fargo held her off, concentrating. She pouted. The men crowding around the table murmured and Fargo stroked his chin as if reconsidering, too late, what he'd done. His opponent's face was made of stone, but Fargo saw the secret smile behind the ice cold eyes. The gambler brought his manicured hand confidently toward his tall pile of coins. The fingers touched the pile, then Fargo saw the hand hesitate as the gambler's eyes glanced up, flickered, and went cold. He suddenly snapped his cards together with a smart click.

"You win," he said to Fargo.

The crowd muttered in disappointment as Fargo took back his pile of money.

"I saw that," a voice said, cutting through the hubbub. "I saw that, little lady." Sally gave a jump, then laughed as if she had accidentally slipped off Fargo's knee. She readjusted herself with a flutter of red silk and lace.

The gambler hastily swept up his money and was starting to rise from the table when a short wiry man with a mop of frizzy silver hair and a long beard pushed his way to the front and grabbed one of the gambler's lapels.

12

In that instant, Sally laughed again nervously and pulled Fargo's hand from her waist upward to cover the soft, full mound of her breast.

"Want to go upstairs now, big man?" she breathed into his ear.

But Fargo pushed her away and slowly stood as he watched the gambler trying to shake off the little man, who had a firm grip on his gleaming white jacket.

"I saw that pretty yellow chicken give you the signal!" the old man shouted at the gambler. "I saw those big eyes blinking at you and don't you deny it!"

Sally's wide blue eyes met Fargo's and he saw the terror in them. She shook her head and then tried a smile on him, but it was guilty as all hell. The crowd was pressing in on them, deadly silent, hanging on every word of the drama. Several of the burly men listening had their hands on their pistols.

"Ridiculous!" the gambler protested. "I deny it, old man. You're seeing things." Sally was trying to slip away, but Fargo reached out and jerked her toward him, then held her pinioned against him.

"What do you say?" he said low in her ear. Sally shook her head no violently, struggling in his powerful hold. He gripped her a little harder.

"Let go of her!" the gambler suddenly shouted, his face livid.

"I told you it wouldn't work," Sally suddenly shrieked at him, sobs in her voice. "I told you we wouldn't get away with it!"

At this the men surrounding the table burst into an uproar. Before Fargo could take a step forward, hands pulled the gambler into the crowd and the contents of his pockets were emptied onto the table. The gambler shouted and struggled but the men hoisted him over their heads and passed him, hand to hand, toward the door.

"Get out," Fargo said quietly to the blond woman cowering beside him. Sally spun about and disappeared into the crowd. A loud laugh came from the other end of the room where, Fargo guessed, the rambunctious crowd had tossed the gambler out the batwing doors and into the muddy street. The gambler's coins and greenbacks were piled on the center of the table.

"Drinks are on me!" Fargo shouted.

The Rusty Bullet crowd roared its approval. Fargo motioned toward the gray-haired man to join him and they sat down at the table as the noise gradually subsided.

Fargo examined the old man before him. A trapper or a prospector maybe. His bright blue eyes were set deep in a face lined with hard living and burned dark by the sun, where it wasn't covered by a scraggly gray beard. His hands were knobby as old apple trees and several fingers were missing their last joints. Bad frostbite, Fargo guessed.

"Name's Skye Fargo," he said. "Much obliged to you." Fargo pushed half the pile of money toward the old man, who eyed it, halved it again, pocketed the smaller pile and pushed the rest back toward Fargo.

"I only take fair pay, what's coming to me," the old man explained. "I've heard of you. My name's Sixty." They shook hands and Fargo ordered a round of beer.

"What kind of name's that?" Fargo asked.

"Sixty-Mile Sam," he answered. "That's my full name. I used to be real good with a dog sled. Took a trip up the Yukon once and made sixty miles a day for nigh on fifteen days." The old man paused a moment, then shook off the memory. "Nobody'd ever done that before. Not since, neither!"

The beer arrived and they raised their mugs, clacked them, and drank down.

"What're you doing so far south?" Fargo asked.

Sixty looked wistful for a moment.

"My brother got sick a few years back so I went on down to Minnesota to visit him. God, it's hot down there. Well, he didn't get better and I stayed with him. Last month he died." Sixty paused and wiped his mouth on his sleeve. His eyes sought Fargo's. "I've been hanging around here trying to think where to go next." He paused again as if remembering something far away. "But that land up there's damn hard on a man," he said softly. "And I'm getting old."

Fargo started to answer when he became aware of a tall man who had come to stand over their table. He glanced up and recognized a face he'd noticed earlier in the crowd, watching the card game. The stranger was powerfully built with a deep chest and long limbs. His brown hair was thick and waved back from a tall square forehead. Two piercing brown eyes looked at him from beneath thick black brows. He wore a dress jacket and a vest with a subtle brocade pattern, a high white collar and no stickpin. Fargo pegged him for a foreigner.

"Excuse me," the gentleman said in a heavy accent. "I've been told that you are Mr. Skye Fargo, the famous Trailsman." Fargo nodded. "May I sit down please to discuss some business?" Fargo indicated a chair and cleared the table of the remaining money as the foreigner seated himself.

"Please allow me to introduce myself," he said. "I am Count Vasili Victoroff. From the Ukraine."

"And this is Sixty-Mile Sam," Fargo put in. The count hardly glanced toward the old man but kept his dark eyes trained on Fargo.

"I have heard you are a remarkable man," Victoroff said. "I have heard you can find trails where no one else can, that you can track down anyone, find anything in the wilderness."

"You bet he can," Sixty put in. "Heard tell he's the best in the business."

"What's the job?" Fargo asked. Count Victoroff laughed heartily.

"*Da, da.* That is what I like so much about you Americans," he said, chuckling. "Always to the point. Now, in Russia, we would take our time. Have some vodka, talk about anything but business." Fargo gestured to the bartender to bring another drink. The count, seeing his gesture, chuckled again.

"So," Fargo said.

"So," the count said slowly, his eyes searching Fargo's face for a long moment. "It's about . . . my daughter." The beer arrived and the count looked at it distastefully, then took a tentative sip. Fargo watched him closely. "Yes, my daughter, Natasha. You see, she was taken from me, kidnapped."

Fargo didn't answer but sat listening and watching the Russian. Sixty caught Fargo's eye and grinned. The count took another sip of the ale.

"How long's she been gone?" Fargo asked.

"Six months," the count said. "And I've been looking for them, for her, ever since."

"And you know who took her?"

"*Da! Da!*" the count's voice rose with suppressed rage. "She was taken right from my villa at my estate! Right out from under my nose by a band of local thugs. Criminals elements of the worst kind." The count paused, his face reddened, and he hit the table with his fist. "It was . . . an outrage!"

"And you've tracked them to America," Fargo said.

"You are a smart man," the count said. "I have found these thieves. *Da,* I have found out where they are hiding with my Natasha. They have a camp far up in the wilderness, in the Russian colony up north. I found out where. Almost where. Now I need someone very good. I am sure you are just the one."

"Sorry," Fargo said. He took a slow swallow of beer and put the mug down on the table, catching the surprised glance from Sixty, who had been closely following the conversation. "Sorry, I'm not your man."

The count sat back in his chair and regarded Fargo for a long moment.

"May I ask why?"

"I have my reasons," Fargo said shortly. The one reason was simple. He had a gut feeling about Count Victoroff. And his gut feeling told him that there was something Victoroff wasn't telling him. And if a man was going to hold out on you from the very beginning, he'd be holding out on you clear to the end. Fargo thought about the girl Natasha for a moment and wondered if she even existed. The tale sounded too incredible to believe. A band of Russian bandits kidnapped a girl and took her halfway around the world?

"Oh, I see the problem," the count said smoothly. He fished around in his coat pocket for a moment and pulled out a very large coin purse. He laid it quietly on the table between them. Fargo didn't even look at it, but just shook his head. The count opened the bag and dumped the coins onto the table with a clatter. Fine gold glittered in the lamplight, dozens of thick coins. Again, Fargo shook his head.

"Sorry about your daughter," Fargo said slowly. "I'm sure you can find somebody else to help you."

The count's eyes went dull and he gathered the gold back into the purse.

"I see I have misjudged you," he said. He bowed stiffly and walked away. When he had gone, Sixty chuckled.

"Don't like Russians?"

"Just a feeling," Fargo said. "About that one."

The fat bartender came by with a loaded tray and put two beers down on the table and a big tab for the round of beers for everybody. Fargo paid up with the gambler's money and as the bartender started to leave, he pulled up short and turned back, putting the tray down. He patted his vest pocket and extracted an envelope.

"Oh, Mr. Fargo," he said. "I meant to give you this when you came in tonight. It arrived on the afternoon mail run."

Fargo took the envelope. It was tattered and had been pasted over with many stamps. His name was printed in big awkward capital letters. He opened it and read:

You sed cal if I ever needed help. I do. Come to Alakanuk. Theyrs meny men might dye. Yr old frind, MacKenzie.

Fargo read the words several times and then looked at the date of the message—two months before. He swore under his breath.

"Trouble?" Sixty asked.

"Sounds like it," Fargo said. "Up north around the Yukon, your old stomping ground. Old friend, name of Pete MacKenzie."

"MacKenzie!" Sixty squawked. "The hell you say! Pete's in trouble?"

"You know him?"

"Put his first moss diaper on him," Sixty said proudly. "Taught that boy to read the snow myself. Watched him kill his first bear. Haven't seen little Petie-Boy in years." Fargo smiled at the nickname, remembering the huge dark hulk of Pete MacKenzie. "What kind of trouble is it?"

"He doesn't say." Fargo handed him the piece of paper and Sixty bent over it for several minutes, patiently sounding out the letters. Then he nodded and sat back. They looked at one another.

"I guess I'm going up to the Yukon after all," Fargo said.

"I'm with you," the old man said. "If you're a-willing."

19

Fargo lifted his glass in answer.

"Here's to Petie," Sixty said solemnly.

They clanked the beer mugs together, drank up, and left the bar together.

A week later, Fargo stood on the deck of the schooner and gazed at the dense gray fog. From time to time it cleared and he could glimpse the towering cliffs and distant blue mountains of Russian America. Here and there massive glaciers, frozen rivers of ice, wound between the peaks toward the sea.

"The captain informs me we'll be arriving at Alakanuk in a few minutes," a voice said. Fargo glanced at Count Victoroff, who had walked up from behind him. Fargo nodded wordlessly and looked out at the leaden water again as the count moved away.

For a week, they'd been on the ship as it made its way up the northwest coast. Several times, the count had tried again to persuade Fargo to take on the trailblazing job. But Fargo had simply answered that he had other business to take care of and finally Victoroff had given up.

A break between the drifting banks of clouds showed a wide inlet—the mouth of the mighty Yukon. With a creak, the boat turned. The white sails snapped in the steady wind and soon the fog lifted. As they sailed into the inlet, Fargo spotted a tiny collection of dwellings on the snow-dappled barren bank. That was the village of Alakanuk. All hands were on deck to lower the sails and within minutes the ship was easing in toward the dock.

Sixty appeared from below hauling their bags of gear and they disembarked.

There was no hotel in Alakanuk but Fargo spotted a sign that said ROOMS TO RENT and Sixty stayed to arrange accommodations while Fargo went to scout out the town and ask around for MacKenzie. As he wandered through the tiny village, Fargo spotted fur-jacketed Russian trappers hurrying along in the biting wind, but few Indians. Most were probably out fishing. Ever since the Russians had sailed into the straits two hundred years before, their trappers, the *promyshlenniki*, had ravaged the Indian tribes—the Inuit on the coast and the Ingalik, Tanana, and Koyukon tribes of the interior, sometimes holding hostages in exchange for furs. An uneasy peace had finally come, and in the village of Alakanuk, the Indians and Russians huddled side by side on the barren coast, eking out an existence by trading and whaling.

Alakanuk wasn't much to see—a few lumber buildings, a general store which also housed the town bar and post office, a row of sod houses, and the low sod mounds which were the roofs of Inuit dwellings half buried in the earth. He knew the round houses were constructed of whalebone and driftwood sunk into the ground beneath the domes of thick sod. A few Inuit kayaks, called *baidarkas*, lined the rocky beach. At one end of the village stood a Russian church, the onion-shaped dome as gray as the sky.

At the other end was a sprawling camp of more than two dozen dirty canvas tents, pitched in the snow and mud. Fargo walked between the tents and looked about. A couple dozen men were loafing around by the campfires playing cards or whittling. Several were cleaning rifles. They were a tough-looking bunch, hard-eyed, many with scarred faces and missing fingers where the hard living of the north had left its mark on them. Suddenly, he saw a familiar figure approaching, picking his way through the mud and talking to a heavy-set bald man with a long black beard. Count Victoroff paused when he spotted Fargo and hurried forward. He wore a full-length beaver coat and thick fur hat, Russian style.

"Mr. Fargo! This is my army," the count said grandly, gesturing around him. "And you see we are well supplied." He swept a hand toward where dozens of sled dogs were staked and piles of provisions awaited loading onto a row of dog sleds. "This is Skye Fargo, the one I was telling you about," the count said to the bald man beside him. The man looked at Fargo curiously and then reluctantly extended his hand, which was hard and callused.

"I'm Bull Slade," he said. "Head of this outfit." Fargo nodded. "Heard you're a good trailblazer. We could use a good tracker." Fargo shrugged and the count cut in.

"Mr. Fargo knows my offer still stands," the count said.

"Yeah," Fargo responded. "Good luck to you." He moved away from them before the count could press him again. At the edge of the camp, he spotted two men leaning against a pile of broken rock. He hailed them.

"Been up here in Alakanuk long?" he asked.

The taller one grunted.

The other said, "Long enough," and tucked some tobacco in his cheek.

"You ever run into a fellow named MacKenzie?" At his name both men jumped a little. "I'm looking for him."

"Why?" the short one asked, eyes cold.

"Met him a long time ago," Fargo said. The two men looked at each other.

"Yeah, we know him. MacKenzie was supposed to be leading this outfit," one of them said. He chewed his plug a long moment. "But now he ain't."

"How come?" Fargo asked, his thoughts whirling. So Pete MacKenzie had been mixed up in the count's rescue mission.

"Ain't you heard? Pete MacKenzie got himself killed," the man said. He turned and spat a yellow stream of tobacco into a snowbank. "Last week."

Fargo glanced across the gray water of the bay for a long moment. Pete MacKenzie dead. "What the hell happened?" Fargo asked.

"Enemies, I guess. Or a woman," one said with a shrug. He spat again. "That's what they say. But who knows?"

"He'd just come back from a solo trip upriver," the other said. "Trying to find this Russian big shot's daughter. I heard he figured out where she's hid, pretty much. Then he got killed. They're looking around now for another tracker."

"How'd he die?"

"Go see for yourself," one said. "You'll find him five miles west of here. By the bend of the creek," one said. "What's left of him."

After another moment of silence, Fargo walked

away. Snow blew in and was beginning to fall, obscuring the hills to the west. He walked into the general store, picked out some sturdy snowshoes, strapped them on, and started up the creek. He had gone several miles before he thought of Sixty but it was too late to turn back and fetch him. Instead, Fargo tramped on through the falling snow, to find whatever was left of Pete MacKenzie. And afterward, he'd call on Count Victoroff and find out what the hell was really going on.

"And he found them!" the count said excitedly. "MacKenzie found their secret camp way up the Yukon in the back country, past the Nulato trading post, hidden in the hills."

"So, then you know where they are. Why do you need a tracker?" Fargo asked. Sixty shifted beside him. They were sitting at one of the wooden tables at one side of the general store, which was what passed for a bar in Alakanuk. The gray morning light filtered through the small dirty window.

The count reached into his pocket and pulled out a piece of folded buckskin. He spread it onto the table and Fargo could see that the skin had been marked with berry dye.

"Some kind of map," Sixty said quietly.

"Unfortunately," the count said, "by the time I arrived here, someone had killed him. But he left this map behind."

Fargo made out the familiar shape of the Yukon River, snaking inland, and an "X" at about the spot he knew the Ingalik Indian village of Anvik lay. Further up was a larger "X" where the trading post was and then a series of small dots and pic-

24

tographs of mountains as the trail left the river and turned northwest. Then the markings blurred and the leather was stiff where it had been water-soaked.

"You see, the map was damaged and I can't tell exactly where the camp lies," Victoroff said, tracing the trail with his long finger. My men could wander around in that wilderness for months and still miss them by a few miles. And the snows are coming. In another month, that country will be impassable."

"Why don't you wait until spring?" Sixty asked.

"I can't leave my daughter with those men for another winter," the count said, his eyes blazing. "I can't wait six more months for my revenge. *Nyet*. I need somebody to track them now. I need somebody to go upriver with my men and find that camp. Besides, they won't be expecting an attack this time of year. By spring, they might have moved on."

"So," Fargo said quietly, leaning back in his chair. "Who do you think killed Pete MacKenzie?" Fargo said.

The count looked toward the window, where the snow was starting to fall against the gray sky.

"Isn't it obvious?" Victoroff said, anger seething under his words. "Those thugs. Those criminals who are holding Natasha discovered MacKenzie knew where they were hiding. Maybe they have friends here in Alakanuk. Or maybe they followed him down the Yukon. In any case, he got back alive and then a day later, he disappeared. They are dangerous men. Evil men." The count's brows

25

lowered and he looked again at Fargo. "I will hunt them down if it's the last thing I do."

Fargo thought of MacKenzie's frozen corpse hanging from the spruce. And the words of MacKenzie's last message came back to him. That must have been what his message meant—he needed Fargo to come and help with the assault on the Russian gang's hideout. Otherwise, many men, the count's men, would die.

"I'll help you," Fargo said.

The count smiled broadly, pulled out the poke of gold coins, and threw them down on the table.

"Pete MacKenzie was an old friend of mine," Sixty said heartily. "So, I'm coming too." Fargo noticed that the smile on the count's face flickered for a moment.

"You . . . *knew* Mr. MacKenzie?" Victoroff asked, a slight strain in his voice.

"Why sure," Sixty said. "Everybody in the Yukon knew Pete MacKenzie." Victoroff's face relaxed.

"*Da, Da,*" he said with a laugh.

Fargo felt the slight uneasiness prick him again, the vague idea that everything was not right about this whole deal. And he decided not to tell the count about MacKenzie's message to him. For a moment, he reconsidered taking the job. But now he'd said he'd go. And, damn it, he had to find MacKenzie's killer. Taking the job that MacKenzie was supposed to have done might be the only way to figure out who'd killed him.

Fargo and Sixty rose and left the general store. Outside, a blast of bitter wind swirled the snow around them. Fog was moving in toward shore. Sixty raised his head and sniffed the wind.

"It's only October and the snow's coming hard on the coast already," he said, shaking his head. "It's going to be a bad winter. Real bad."

As he followed Sixty toward the camp of the count's men, Fargo glanced toward the hills, partly obscured by the driving snow. Up the Yukon was the most dangerous territory in the world, cold, heartless, and hungry. It would freeze the life out of a man if it could and every minute out there was a struggle for survival. It would take everything he knew just to get by and a helluva lot of luck to find out what he wanted to know. A hard blast of wind roared around them and Sixty pulled up short a moment and squinted as his eyes too searched inland for the hills obliterated by the blowing snow.

"In winter, that territory's meaner than a starving wolf with his teeth sunk in your leg," Sixty muttered under his breath as if reading Fargo's thoughts. They turned toward the camp.

2

The next day, Fargo and Sixty kept busy getting outfitted for the trek up the Yukon. With the advance pay from Count Victoroff, they headed to the general store. Sixty bought extra pairs of snowshoes netted with the rawhide straps called babiche. Fargo picked out a pair of fur-lined leggings with attached moccasins and then asked to see the parkas. The store owner, weary-eyed, spoke with a heavy Russian accent.

"I got such parkas. You wait here," he said, disappearing into a room behind the counter. In a moment he returned with several of the Ingalik-made jackets, fur-lined, hooded and essential for Arctic travel. Fargo reached for one made of bearskin, to try it on. It fell open and he saw, inside, a circle of stitched skin with the painted face of a red bear, teeth bared. Sixty, standing nearby, reached over and pointed to the image.

"That's unusual," Sixty told Fargo. "The Indian who made this painted that face so the strength of the bear would be given to whoever wears the jacket. That's real good luck." Fargo tried on the jacket, moving his arms and testing its stitched pockets.

"How much for everything?" he asked the Russian. "You take U.S. dollars?" The Russian smiled broadly and ran his practiced eye over the pile of goods on the floor.

"Forty-five," he said, "in dollars." It seemed like a fair price, Fargo thought, accounting for the fact that everything cost more in Russian America. Fargo paid and he and Sixty began collecting everything to carry away.

"You must be going on a long journey," the Russian said, helping them.

"Yeah," Fargo said. "We're going to help Count Victoroff get his daughter back." At that, the Russian froze and his dark eyes grew wide. He swore in Russian under his breath and spit on the floor angrily.

"For you, no forty-five dollars," the Russian said. He tugged on the pile of fur clothing in Sam's arms. "For you, cost three hundred. No, four hundred!"

"What the hell?" Fargo said. He pulled the Russian away and slammed him against the counter. "We've already bought this stuff. And paid for it. You can't raise the price now."

The Russian backed away, muttering under his breath. Fargo and Sixty gathered everything and left the store in a hurry.

"What was that about?" Sixty asked as they walked out into the bitter air.

"Damned if I know," Fargo said. He thought to himself that it seemed as if the Russian had got upset when he discovered they were working for Count Victoroff. But the count was Russian too. So why would that matter to the shopkeeper?

The wind was a steady blast from the ocean. The bearskin parka kept the cold out completely. It was almost too hot, Fargo thought, but he knew that wouldn't be the case when they got up the Yukon where it could get down around 80 degrees below zero.

Back at camp, Fargo and Sixty headed toward the dog sleds. There Bull Slade was directing the loading of the supplies. He spotted them coming.

"That's yours," he said gruffly, pointing to a small light sled. The sled would carry both of them but not much else. "We'll haul the heavy supplies," Bull added, seeing the question in Fargo's eyes. "And once we get close to those bandits' camp, you'll be on foot anyway." Fargo looked back at the small sled. It didn't make a lot of difference if they all stuck together. But what if he and Sixty got separated from the rest and had no supplies?

"No," Fargo said. "We need a bigger sled." Bull turned toward him, eyes fiery above his black beard. He swept the cap off his bald head and Fargo could see the flush creep up his scalp.

"What do you mean, no?" Bull said. His short temper had ignited and it was clear he was a man who was used to being obeyed without question.

"No," Fargo said again. "I want one bigger. And we'll haul our own supplies." Bull's face turned livid.

"You'll take the sled I say you'll take," he said, his voice quivering with rage. "I'm in charge of this outfit, Mr. Big Shot Trailsman. And don't you forget it." Bull took a menacing step forward.

"This isn't worth a fight," Fargo warned, his

voice low, his big hands in fists, ready for a move from Bull Slade.

"The hell it's not," Slade said. "I'm the boss here. That's worth fighting over." Bull suddenly lashed out and Fargo neatly blocked his arm with an upward thrust, then brought his right hard into Slade's belly.

"Stop! Stop this!" Count Victoroff shouted, hurrying toward them. Fargo stepped back from Bull Slade, who hunched over, darting angry looks. "What is this about?"

Fargo turned to face the count. "Sixty and I need a bigger sled," he explained. "This one's not big enough to carry supplies. If we get separated from the rest of you, it would make a difference between life and death. Slade here seemed to have a problem with that."

"He'll take the sled I give him," Slade muttered under his breath. "I'm boss here." Victoroff looked from Fargo to Slade and back again and then at the sled.

"I see your point, Mr. Fargo, take a larger one," the count said. Slade turned angrily and stalked away, glancing over his shoulder at Fargo. Well, he'd made an enemy of Bull Slade, but it couldn't be helped. Fargo and Sixty turned to examine the row of sleds.

"This one is mine," Count Victoroff said, pointing to a high graceful sled of whalebone with caribou runners. Fargo and Sixty chose a long and low wooden sled with a sturdy double webbing of babiche.

"How about dogs?" Fargo asked.

"Take your pick," the count said. He pointed

them toward where the dogs were staked and then walked away toward the village.

Fargo looked over the area of trampled snow, where dozens of wolf dogs were staked, Indian style. The half-wild sled dogs would chew through any rope or rawhide leash in a matter of minutes, so the natives had devised a rawhide collar attached to a wooden pole. At the other end of the pole, out of the reach of the wolf dog's sharp teeth was another rawhide thong fastened to a stake driven in the ground. The dog could walk around and around in a circle but could not get free. Fargo and Sixty looked over the collection of wolf dogs.

"That one," Fargo said at last, pointing to a huge and muscular smoke gray dog with rough bristling fur that marked it as mostly wolf. It lay watching them warily with yellow eyes that shone with intelligence.

"Good choice for a leader," Sixty agreed. Fargo headed toward the wolf dog, which tensed at his approach, eyes unblinking. This was the moment, Fargo knew, when the dog would learn who was in charge. With all his senses alert, Fargo stepped across the circumference, into the dog's staked circle. Without a sound, the wolf dog sprang toward him, a flash of fur and long bared teeth. Instantly, Fargo stepped back and the dog's leap was suddenly arrested by the pull of the wooden pole. The wolf dog yelped, fell short, and landed in the snow, fury in its eyes. For a moment, they stood looking at one another, man and dog.

Fargo felt in his pocket for a small piece of pemmican. He held it out, beyond the dog's reach. The wolf dog's nostrils twitched. Suddenly, Fargo tossed it to the far side of the staked circle. The dog sprang after it and, just as quickly, Fargo hopped into the center of the circle beside the stake. The dog gobbled the tidbit and whirled about, furious to see Fargo inside its territory, but unable to get close to him because of the wooden pole. It circled him, growling low. Fargo wrenched the stake from the ground and held on to the pole. The gray dog rushed him again, teeth snapping, but Fargo thrust the wooden pole outward, holding the dog well out of striking distance. Again and again, in a rage, it tried to get at him to no avail. Sixty laughed at the spectacle.

Finally, the wolf dog tired and sat down with a whimper, yellow eyes softening. It was defeated. Fargo felt in his pocket and found another piece of the pemmican. This time, the wolf dog's demeanor was completely different. Its tail beat the snow and it whined. Fargo threw the meat and the dog ate it, then sat again, looking expectantly at Fargo.

"That long-tooth knows who's master now," Sixty said. "He'll make a good lead dog." Fargo warily approached the dog, maintaining his grasp on the pole, but the dog remained complacent, tail wagging. Fargo loosed the pole from its neck, and felt the thick fur ruff around the dog's neck.

"We'll call him Long-Tooth," Fargo said. He drove the stake into the ground near their sled and walked away. This time, he noticed, the wolf dog followed him with its eyes and remained still.

Fargo and Sixty spent another hour looking over the dogs and picking nine more for their team. Over and over, Fargo was reminded of the uneasy alliance that existed between the men and the wolf dogs which hauled the sleds. The wild dogs only responded to brutality of strength and superior human cunning. For a moment, he thought of his trusty pinto back in the stable in Vancouver and wished he'd brought it along. But Russian America was horse-killing country. The only way to travel in winter was with the wolf dogs. But you had to keep an eye on them every minute.

In midafternoon, Sixty and Fargo packed their food and equipment onto the sled, lashing it low and tight with ropes of braided babiche. The other men in the camp were also loading their sleds and preparing to move out in the morning. Fargo spotted the two men he'd seen the day before who had told him about Pete MacKenzie. They were trying to steady a tall pile of supplies as they tied it onto their sled.

"Need a hand?" Fargo said, walking over. The two men ignored him. He stood watching as they tied the final knots. They had done it badly. On the first curve of the trail, the top-heavy sled would topple over and the caravan would have to stop until the sled could be repacked. "This sled is loaded wrong," Fargo said. "You packed it too tall."

The two men turned and glowered at him.

"What's it to you?" one said, spitting a stream of yellow tobacco juice into the snow.

"I'm trailblazing for this outfit and I don't want to call a halt tomorrow while you pick your Sunday long johns out of the snowbank curve," Fargo said.

"I'll give the orders here, Mr. Fargo," Bull Slade's voice cut in.

Fargo shrugged and headed back toward Sixty. It was going to be a damned uncooperative group, starting with Bull Slade. The best thing to do was just keep out of the way and do his job. He and Sixty finished packing and headed off to supper and their last night in a real bed. As they passed the long line of loaded sleds, Fargo noticed that the two men had done as he'd suggested. The sled's contents were packed low and tight now.

Dawn glowed dimly above the southeastern horizon as they made final preparations to pull out of Alakanuk. Where the tents had been was a stretch of muddy trampled snow where a few campfires still smoldered. Men scurried around and the sled dogs were barking and howling at the chaos.

One by one, Fargo and Sixty led the dogs into their traces and watched as Long-Tooth, in the lead harness, subdued the other wolf dogs with snapping teeth and menacing growls. Count Victoroff appeared in his tall fur hat and seated himself in his sled beneath a bearskin lap robe. Bull Slade took his place at the front of the count's sled, long whip in hand. By the time the sleds were ready to move out, dawn was breaking. Fargo took a long gee pole and broke out the runners of the sled, which had frozen to the ground during the night.

"Mush!" Sixty called out, and Long-Tooth and the other nine dogs threw their weight against the harness. The sled jerked forward and then picked up speed. Fargo ran alongside the sled for a way,

35

then slid onto it as the dogs pulled into a steady lope.

With the crack of whips and the whack of the gee poles against the frozen runners, the sleds moved out behind them, as they turned east onto the trail. For the first leg of their journey, the caravan of a dozen sleds would stick to the trail on the south bank of the Yukon, which was broken and well traveled. As they went further inland, the Yukon River would be frozen solid and would provide them with an open road of ice where the stiff wind blew most of the snow away and the sleds could make good time. They would make a three-day run upriver to the Ingalik village of Anvik.

Fargo glanced back to see the last of the small dark houses of Alakanuk disappear behind a low snowy hill and then the flat gray ocean horizon vanished as well. Soon they entered a dark cedar woods and sped along the packed trail. The dog team was pulling well, Fargo noted. Long-Tooth was surefooted and brought the dogs out wide on every curve to avoid overturning the sled and tangling the traces. And in the short downhill runs, Long-Tooth ran ahead, keeping the traces taut so the dogs at the rear weren't nipped by the speeding sled.

At midday, they called a halt on the bank of the Yukon. Here, the river was a wide white flat, dark in spots where water still bubbled up over the fresh winter ice. Fargo strode out onto the river, listening to the creak beneath his moccasins, his eyes searching the river's expanse and measuring the width of the dark patches of wetness. He knelt and brushed away the fresh powder from the sur-

36

face of the frozen Yukon. Below, through the clear star ice, he saw the dark bubbles of the rushing current. The ice was too thin to risk it. But further inland, maybe another day's travel, as they gained the higher elevations, it would be thicker. He headed back to the bank and motioned for them to continue on the trail.

By nightfall, the wind had picked up hard. Here in the north country, the light didn't linger in the sky long after the distant white sun had set far to the southwest. They held to the trail for another long cold hour and then Fargo called a halt at the edge of a wide meadow under the shelter of some tall spruce trees. The sleds pulled up into a tight double circle and the men hopped out and stretched their cold aching muscles. Bull Slade gave orders for a detail to search for firewood and the rest fell to unhitching and feeding the dog teams.

Sixty loosened the traces of their team while Fargo portioned out the package of moose meat for the first day's rations, tossing each gobbet to the next dog. After each dog had been fed, they raced off in a pack with the other sled dogs and Fargo could hear them barking in the woods. It was impractical and dangerous to stake the sled dogs while on the trail. Sometimes a wild wolf pack or a wandering grizzly would rush the camp and a team of staked dogs didn't have a chance of survival. The dogs would run off into the woods a short ways, never straying too far. And they'd return to sleep by the safety of the fire.

Fargo pitched a length of canvas along one side of the loaded sled to make a shelter for the night while Sixty positioned a coffeepot over the roaring fire at the center of camp. In another hour, the sky was dark with scuttling clouds. The sled dogs had returned to camp and each dug a hollow in a snowbank nearby and crept inside to sleep for the night. Sixty and Fargo sat lounging by the crackling fire.

Count Victoroff, a tin mug in one hand and a bottle of vodka in the other, came to sit near them. Far away, a wolf howled, an arcing, lonely sound.

"That sounds like the Ukraine," the count said wistfully.

"You got wolves over there?" Sixty put in.

"*Da, Da.* Wolves, bears, deer. It is beautiful land, the Ukraine." The count's eyes were far away. "On my estate is a forest and a hunting lodge. Lots of wild boar. And golden wheat fields. There is nothing like the sight of Ukraine wheat when the serfs are cutting it . . . "

"Serfs?" Sixty said. "Ain't that like slavery?"

Count Victoroff came out of his reverie and barked a laugh.

"The serfs do not belong to me. They belong to the land," the count said. "Ever since Tsar Boris Gudonov, it has been the law of my country. We boyars and nobility take care of the politics and own the estates. And the serfs take care of the farming. That way, everyone has his place. It is an excellent system. Really, very fair."

Sixty shook his head, unconvinced.

"How long have you been gone from Russia?" Fargo asked.

"For these six months I have been chasing after

those . . . those criminals," the count spat. "And Natasha."

"Why did they kidnap her?" Fargo asked. "For a ransom?"

The count looked puzzled for a moment, then shook his head.

"Ransom? *Nyet, nyet.* They do not ask for money," he said. "I believe they just wanted to make trouble for me. And maybe it is because Natasha is very charming, very beautiful. Long blond hair to her waist and a face like an angel . . ." The count gazed into the fire and was silent.

"Tell me about Natasha's mother," Fargo cut in. "Is she from the Ukraine?" The count's black brows lowered and he stood abruptly.

"I must sleep," he said, his words clipped. "And it is getting late. Please excuse me."

Count Victoroff moved away stiffly toward the white canvas tent that Bull Slade had pitched for him. In a moment he disappeared inside. Fargo exchanged glances with Sixty and then sat for a moment looking after the count thinking that there was something strange about the whole affair. The night wind suddenly blasted flakes against his face. Sixty sniffed the air.

"There's heavy weather coming in," he said, shaking his grizzled head. "Time to turn in."

Fargo and Sixty scrubbed their tin plates and cups with snow and turned in for the night. Fargo slid beneath the canvas, which was pitched against the downward side of the packed sled. He wrapped himself in bearskin robes. As he drifted off to sleep, he saw a woman with long blond hair.

* * *

In the darkness, Fargo wondered what had awakened him. He lay still for a moment listening. He heard the slight hiss of the snow as it fell on the canvas over his head. And the soft whistle of the wind which blew in between the crevices of the loaded sled, which formed the other side of his sleeping quarters. Then he heard it again. A low grunt. Not human.

Fargo grabbed his Sharps rifle and sprang from the tent into the cold night air. In the darkness, he could see the outlines of the camp, the circle of sleds, canvas sheathed, covered with falling snow. And emerging from the dark trees was a hulking blackness, heading straight for the sleds. In an instant, the air was filled with a raucous howling and barking of the dogs as their noses detected the intruder and they burst out of the snowbanks where they had been sleeping.

The huge grizzly rose to its full height at the same moment Fargo raised his rifle and squeezed off a shot. An instant later, he knew he'd aimed too high. The bullet had lodged in the shoulder and the bear was only wounded. The retort echoed and the camp was suddenly awake with men shouting and scrambling for their rifles. The wounded bear bellowed and was quickly surrounded by a circle of yammering dogs who rushed in and nipped at its heels. It was impossible to get a clear shot without killing one of the dogs.

Fargo ran closer to the enraged animal just as it took a swipe with one huge paw and lifted one of the sled dogs into the air. The dog yelped in agony as it was tossed into the snow and Fargo fired again, straight into the heart. The bear shuddered, took a slow swipe at another dog, missed, and sank down into the snow. Instantly, Fargo finished him off with a final shot through the skull. The dogs swarmed over the dying bear, tearing at the fur to get to the fresh meat. The rest of the men, wide awake now, rushed the dogs, and beat them with the butts of their rifles until they drove them off the huge carcass.

"Helluva bear," Sixty said appreciatively.

"Congratulations, Mr. Fargo," the count said grandly, coming up behind them. "You must come hunting with me on my estate in the Ukraine sometime." He took a look at the bear and then retreated back to his tent. Bull Slade sulked by the blackened firepit and a couple of men rekindled the campfire.

While the others held the whining dogs at bay, Fargo pulled a knife from his belt and began taking the skin off with quick motions. Steam rose in the freezing air. At the smell of the fresh blood, the dogs tried to rush in again but the men drove them back. Sixty grasped one end of the wet skin and pulled as Fargo loosened it with quick slicing strokes. Once the huge pelt came free, they carried it off while the other men fell to hacking the haunches of the bear.

Once clear of the circle of slavering dogs, Fargo and Sixty rolled up the bearskin. The skin would freeze, which would preserve it for the moment. When they got to the trading post at Nulato, they could trade the raw pelt. They finished lashing the rolled skin to their sled and returned to help with the butchering.

In an hour, the bloody, steaming slabs of bear meat—the shoulders and haunches, along with the liver and tongue—had been hacked apart and stowed in canvas bags among the various sleds. The bear paws were chopped off with a hatchet for trading to the Indians. Strips of meat hung sizzling over the blazing campfire. Finally, at Fargo's signal, the men retreated from the bloody carcass and the dogs rushed in to finish the job. In a moment, the spot where the bear had fallen was a mass of writhing dogs quarreling over the meat, their teeth tearing at the head and scraps of skin, cracking the bones, their tongues even lapping up the bloodstained snow.

"Hell, you'd think they hadn't eaten in a month," Fargo said.

"Smart dogs," Sixty said. "Eat while you can. As much as you can. That's the way of the north country."

Daylight wasn't far off. Breakfast was as much bear meat as you could eat and strong black coffee. Many of the men raised their tin cups to Fargo while Bull Slade shot him dirty looks. The snow was sweeping into the camp now in earnest, hissing into the fire and driving the men close around the yellow flames. They didn't linger, but each took a hearty portion of roasted meat which would be eaten cold at midday and went to put the dogs back into the traces.

With all the snow clouds, there wouldn't be a dawn, Fargo thought as he called out to Long-Tooth. Just a very gradual lightening of the white sky as the sun began its low arc far to the south. The gray wolf dog came reluctantly toward Fargo, its tongue lolling and belly full. It had eaten well and now it wanted to crawl back into the snowbank and sleep it off. But it was time to move on. Fargo fastened the harness around Long-Tooth and stood. The dog licked his hand.

Soon the rest of the teams were assembled and in the traces. Fargo broke out the runners and ran alongside as the sled got under way. They made good time racing through the gray light. The trail, softened with fresh snow, was still hardpacked underneath and the dogs pulled well. By midmorning the sky was bright white and the trail dipped down parallel to the wide expanse of the frozen Yukon. Once again, Fargo walked across the ice, brushed aside the snow, and saw the river rushing below. Still too close. Midstream was a patch of black open water where the ice hadn't closed up yet and the rim ice was sure to be thin and dangerous. Too risky, he decided. He walked back toward where the sleds waited.

"We'd make better time on the ice," Bull Slade called out to him.

"Still too thin," Fargo said. The sleds started up again and they continued up the snowy trail.

At midday the blizzard increased and the dark spruce were dim around them, the hills turned into shadows in the blowing snow. The dogs were tiring and as the snow deepened on the trail, the sleds became harder to pull. Fargo realized they'd have to start breaking the trail on snowshoes for the sleds to pass. They halted again. Fargo strapped on snowshoes and preceded the caravan, striding through the soft powder between the trees. They continued through the long afternoon

43

hours and Fargo felt the weariness come over him as he fought against the blasting wind, keeping his legs moving against the soft white resistance of the snow. Again the trail dipped toward the river and Fargo glanced across it longingly. Maybe one more day of freeze, he thought and they could chance it. Suddenly he heard a shout behind him and he turned to see that Bull Slade had whipped his dog team and turned the count's sled off the trail and was descending toward the river.

Bull laughed defiantly as he saw Fargo's startled face and the sled skittered onto the ice. With a shout, the next sled followed, then another, and the entire line was heading onto the wide flat expanse of frozen river. Fargo watched as Bull led the caravan speeding upriver.

"What the hell's he been doing?" Sixty muttered.

"Trying to be a big man," Fargo spat.

"He'll get somebody killed," Sixty said, shaking his head.

There was nothing he could do but follow, he realized. He climbed onto the sled and took over driving the team while Sixty sat in the rear.

"Mush!" Fargo called out and Long-Tooth moved forward with the rest of the dogs and they drew a wide circle down the gentle slope, then bumped out onto the ice.

The wind had blown off most of the snow off the river ice, except for a couple of rough icy layers that provided traction for the dogs, while the runners sliced through the snow to the ice below, which was slick and fast. The dogs ran joyfully, energetically, freed from pulling against the weight of the thick drifts. Still, Fargo did not trust the ice.

They had gone scarcely two miles and were rounding a huge curve when Fargo saw it far up ahead, a wide patch of unevenness barely covered by the new snow. Another man might not have noticed the slight darkness of the area, but Fargo did, and knew it spelled trouble. He shouted to Bull Slade, but the whistling wind carried his voice away while the sleds raced forward. Fargo cracked the whip and drove the dogs to a flat-out racing run, pulling alongside the other sleds and passing them.

They were going faster and faster now, Fargo shouting at Slade to hold up. Bull Slade turned around at the sound of his voice and saw Fargo gaining on him. Slade grinned and whipped his dogs to go faster, thinking Fargo was trying to move into the lead position again. Instead of looking ahead of him, Slade was now concentrating on whipping his dogs and measuring Fargo's progress. Then Fargo spotted a dark gap of water. They were racing straight toward it, nearer and nearer. Fargo swore and shouted again, gesticulating. Count Victoroff heard him and looked around, then saw the dark patch before them. The count half rose in the sled and shouted at Bull Slade.

Slade spotted the thin ice now and turned his dog team hard right toward the shore. Fargo, running fast beside the second sled in line, pulled hard on his own team to halt them just as the second sled shot past.

Fargo heard the sharp crack of the ice breaking. The two men on board scrambled across the top of the sled in a panic to jump off. But it was too late. The second sled tipped sideways and slid off a chunk of ice into the black hole of river. A few of the dogs bobbed up among the chunks of ice, yelping for a scant instant, and then they were sucked down into the eddying water as the swiftly moving current of the Yukon River swept them away, underneath the ice. The sled, two men, and a whole team of dogs had just disappeared.

Fargo pulled hard again on his team. Sixty shouted. The dogs had their nails dug into the ice as the team and the sled slid toward the black water and Fargo heard the ice crack again, this time right beneath him. They were going in.

3

The dark choppy water gaped before them and the dogs yelped, their nails scratching the ice as they tried desperately to halt. With a splash, Long-Tooth slid into the water, followed by two more dogs. The sled was still sliding forward. Fargo heard the crack of ice below the runners of the sled and he realized there was only one thing to do. He twisted around and grabbed Sixty's coat. Together, they rolled off the sled onto the ice, hitting it stretched out. Fargo rolled once, then reached and made a blind grab for the runner of the sled as it shot past him, pulled by the weight of the dogs falling into the open water.

His gloved hand caught an edge of the runner and he held on, bringing up his other hand to hold tight. The weight of the sled, now tilting into the river, was dragging him toward the hole. The dogs were bobbing and yelping with the pain of the freezing water. He was being dragged facedown across the wet ice toward the river while he held onto the sled. An instant later, he felt a pull on his ankle and knew Sixty, spread-eagle on the ice behind him, had grabbed hold.

Still they continued sliding toward the water.

The sled was heavier than the two of them. For a moment, Fargo considered letting go but there was still a small chance of saving the dogs. If he let go, the sled would go in and drag the dogs straight under. He heard the shouting of the other men behind him.

Inch by inch, they were dragged forward. Fargo's shoulders ached with the pull of the sled's weight. The dogs, still in their traces, paddled and tried desperately to scramble out of the water, but their forepaws broke the edge of the ice. Fargo watched as Long-Tooth got his paws onto a thicker rim and got himself half out, only to be dragged back down into the water by the traces which bound him to the other paddling dogs.

Forgo swore. The sled gave another lurch forward and pain shot through Fargo's shoulders as he held on. He glanced behind him to see several of the men from the other sleds, hesitating to move closer. "Down on your bellies!" he shouted. "Get in a chain!"

One of the men grasped what he meant and lay down, moving slowly forward on the thin ice, reaching toward Sixty's ankle. Another man did the same behind him. In another moment, Fargo felt himself being pulled backward toward the thicker ice. He held onto the sled.

"Let it go!" one of the men behind him yelled. "Let the sled go!" Fargo glanced at the dogs in the black water. They were whimpering now, shivering, and still trying desperately to scramble onto the ice, falling back again and again.

"Pull harder!" Fargo yelled back. "We can do it!"

He felt the tug on his ankle again and he flexed

his strong arms, bringing the sled down flat on its runners. Then he felt himself being dragged slowly back across the ice and he and the sled began to slide away from the dark water. Hand over hand, Fargo pulled the sled back toward him until the back runner of the sled was within Sixty's reach.

"Grab the sled!" he shouted to Sixty. "I'll get the dogs loose."

Sixty made a grab for the sled while Fargo inched forward again. The ice beneath him was rotten and covered with water. The cold burned him and the wind whipped his face. The rawhide traces which tied the dogs to the sled were taut. Fargo slipped the knife from his ankle holster and pulled himself up slowly to one elbow, careful not to put too much weight on the thin ice in any one spot. He sawed at one rawhide thong until it finally gave way. The sled jerked backward and was held by the other side of the harness. He sawed at it too but the water had frozen it solid, making it all the harder to cut. Finally, it too parted and suddenly the sled gave a lurch backward, freed from the weight of the dogs in the water.

The ice groaned again and the water on it deepened. Fargo was numb all over. The fiercely cold wind bit him.

"Come on, Fargo!" the men shouted. "Come on back!"

Fargo glanced again at the dogs in the water. They were too cold to move now. What remaining strength they had they were using to keep their frozen paws on top of the edge of the ice and their noses above the dark water. If one of them gave up and went down, they'd all go under. Long-Tooth looked at him with desperate yellow eyes and Fargo heard the men calling behind him to save himself.

"Toss me a rope!" he yelled over his shoulder. He inched forward again across the wet ice until he reached the very edge of the black water. He threw off his icy gloves and, knife in hand, plunged his fist into the water. The burning cold made him gasp. He felt numbly alongside Long-Tooth's harness for the trace line and began cutting.

Now the black anger rose in him. He cursed Bull Slade for his stupidity in heading across the ice and felt the hot anger giving him strength. The cold was gone now. He felt nothing but the fire of anger and the burning fury. The trace line parted.

Sixty had crept within two yards of him and thrown a rope with a loop at the end. Fargo slipped the rope around Long-Tooth's neck and pulled on the dog's frozen fur just as Sixty tugged on the rope. Long-Tooth whimpered once, then with a last effort, scrambled up on the ice rim. It held and, shivering, the dog limped toward the shouting men. Fargo felt the ice give way beneath his elbows and he moved back as the rim collapsed a few feet more and the dogs paddled, helplessly.

One by one, with Sixty's help, Fargo pulled the dogs from the dark water. After the last one came up he slid himself backward over the wet ice, away from the black water hole that had swallowed one sled and had almost got two. When he reached the firmer ice, he got to his feet. The bitter wind had frozen the water in his clothing and his flesh burned. Sixty came up and clapped him on the back, but Fargo hardly noticed. He only had eyes for Bull Slade, standing on the shore, his back turned, talking to some of his men. Fargo headed straight for Bull.

The men saw him coming and stepped back from Bull, who whirled around to see what was the matter. Bull Slade's jaw dropped with surprise.

"Two men died out there," Fargo said, his voice a growl.

"And you rode right into the river, Trailsman," Bull Slade shot back.

"Trying to keep you from going in," Fargo retorted. Despite himself, he was shivering violently.

"Let's get one thing straight," Bull said. "I'm head of this outfit."

"And I'm doing the trailblazing," Fargo said. "Two men, a team of dogs, and a sled of supplies lost in the river. The ice was too goddamn thin. From now on, we go where I say, when I say."

"I give the orders here, Fargo," Bull shot back. The burly man brought his arm upward, but despite his shivering, Fargo was too fast. He brought his fist up hard in a powerful punch to Slade's jaw. Slade flew backward and landed in a snowbank. Fargo was too cold to feel much of anything. He didn't stop but continued on, climbing up the bank toward the two roaring yellow fires where the men were keeping the wet dogs running around and around in a close circle so they wouldn't die of exposure before they'd dried out.

Some distance away from the fire, Count Victoroff was strapping on showshoes and talking to a group of men who were loading up with rifles. Looked like a hunting party, Fargo thought as they moved off. The count caught sight of him and came over.

"Mr. Fargo," the count said warmly. Fargo beat his chest to break the thick coat of ice and began to peel off his frozen wet clothes. "My thanks to you for quick thinking. Without your warning, Mr. Slade and I would have gone in."

Fargo glanced up at the count for a second but continued peeling off his frozen garments, standing as close to the fire as he dared.

"Well, your man Slade hasn't got the picture yet," Fargo said. "Am I leading this caravan or is he?"

"Oh, you are, certainly," Count Victoroff said. He pulled on his fur hat worriedly. "I will have a word with Mr. Slade. *Da, da.* Leave him to me."

Fargo ignored the count as he moved off and concentrated on his fingers and toes. Yeah, he could still feel them. Good sign, but they were stinging hot with pain. It would be hours before he and the dogs would be dried out and ready to go on. By then it would be almost nightfall. Bull Slade's mistake had cost them half a day's time, the loss of a sled, a dog team, and two men.

Fargo stripped down and rubbed himself with a dry blanket. Sixty held some dry clothes by the fire and handed them to him, toasty warm. Then the old man pulled up a crate and Fargo sat while Sixty massaged some hot bear grease into his feet and hands.

"Lucky you didn't lose a few digits," Sixty said. "I've seen that river take a lot of men and parts of men." He held up his right hand and wiggled the stump of his pinky. "That old Yukon took two joints of this one time. Yes, she did."

"Thanks for holding on to me," Fargo said, wincing at the pain in his feet as Sixty rubbed them gently.

"Holding on! Hell, I wouldn't have missed the show! I never seen a man pull a whole dog team out of the jaws of the Yukon," Sixty said, chuckling. "One dog, maybe." They glanced over to the other fire where the men were driving the wet dogs around and around the flames, keeping them moving near the radiant warmth.

Two hours later, Fargo felt thoroughly warmed. Or as warm as anyone could get out on the Yukon trail. In any case, his blood was running in his hands and feet. The dogs had dried out and dark was coming on. All afternoon, Bull Slade sulked angrily about, shooting furious looks at Fargo and stroking his jaw. The men had pulled the sleds up and pitched camp around the fire. The count, having taken several of the men off on a hunting foray, returned empty-handed and silent. He sat staring into the fire and drinking from his vodka flask.

Fargo pulled on dry leggings and a parka and moved away from the fire to help Sixty make camp. While the old man kept the rest of the dogs at bay, Fargo fed their exhausted team an extra ration of bear. Long-Tooth licked Fargo's hand as it had the day before, then turned and wolfed down the portion of half-frozen flesh. Then the dog team dug holes into the snow and bedded down early. The other dogs, having only had a half day's run were restless. They sprang off into the forest.

The men were all in a foul mood and they ate the leftover bear meat silently. Just after dinner Count Victoroff, bundled in his long fur coat, called Bull Slade over. The two of them moved away, out of the circle of firelight, into the edge of the spruce forest. Fargo, sitting bundled in a blanket half hidden by the corner of his sled, watched them go, curious to know what they were going to talk about that couldn't be heard by anyone else. When they had passed out of sight, he rose and moved away in the opposite direction as if to check on the dogs.

Then he slipped into the darkness between the black trees and swiftly circled around the camp until he spotted the two men with their backs to him, standing among the trees, facing the fire and talking in low voices. He realized he would have to get very near to overhear their words. He moved forward warily, from trunk to trunk, until he was just a few feet away. He pressed himself against the rough bark trunk and listened.

"That was stupid thing to do, Slade," the count was saying, his voice low.

"Hell, you wanna get there this year, don't you? If I was leading this team we'd be racing up the river."

"If you were in lead we'd all be drowned," the count said. "Mr. Fargo is deciding the trail now. That is why I hired him."

"Look, Victoroff," Bull said defiantly, his voice rising, "I don't work under any two-bit adventurer.

You hired me as head of this outfit. And I rounded up these here men for you.

"*Da, da,*" the count cut in hastily. "You are head of the men. As we agreed. You know why I hired you. But Mr. Fargo is leading on the trail. Surely you understand. That is for the best. For now."

"Yeah," Bull said quietly. "For now."

"You'll get your reward," the count said.

"Yeah," Slade said.

"When we finally find Natasha and those . . . those *peasants*!" Victoroff spoke the word like a curse and he whirled about, moving back toward the campfire. Bull Slade lingered and Fargo, wondering why, stayed where he was. After a few minutes, another man came wandering in among the dark trees.

"You know what we're going to do once we find the girl, don't you?" Slade said to the other man without preamble.

"Sure," the other answered. "We'll kill 'em all. Everybody but us. Including the girl?"

"Including the girl," Slade said. "Just pass the word to be ready at my signal."

Fargo eased himself around the trunk of the tree and watched the dark figures move away, his thoughts whirling. Was Slade going to double-cross the count? Did they mean to kill Natasha? Or was it the count they were talking about? Sixty and Fargo and the count?

Fargo moved silently back through the woods, making a wide circle through the snowy woods, feeling the wind whistle around him. The air was colder now than it had been the night before, bitter and hard, breathtakingly cold.

And he and Sixty and the count were in danger too, Fargo realized. Once they'd served their purpose—finding Natasha and the kidnappers—Bull Slade planned to kill them. But why? Nothing made sense. The campfire was a beckoning yellow glow in the blue darkness. Fargo headed toward it and found Sixty getting ready to bed down. Around them, men were rolled into blankets and huddled under makeshift shelters beside their sleds. The count had turned in for the night but he'd talk to him in the morning.

"You been gone a spell," Sixty observed. "Cavorting with the wolves?"

"I'll tell you tomorrow," Fargo said in a low voice.

"Getting colder," the old man continued nonchalantly, as if Fargo hadn't spoken. Sixty spit into the air and listened. "Nope," he said. "Spittle ain't crackling yet so we're still about fifty below. Let's turn in."

Fargo lay awake under the canvas for a long time, listening to the whistle of the wind and the song of the wolves out in the forest. They were closer tonight. He listened to the howls arcing through the silence of the arctic night.

The sled dogs were out there too, running in the forest. Part wolf and half wild themselves, the dogs would always return as long as the men had meat to feed them. That was the fragile pact between man and dog in the north country. Meat and the safety of a campfire in exchange for pulling the sleds.

But with wolves close by, the dogs wouldn't run far from camp and would stay in a close pack.

They had reason to fear the wild wolves who ran in a hunting pack and who would tear apart any strange wolf dog they found running alone in the forest.

He wondered about Natasha and the men who had kidnapped her. Who were they? And if there was no ransom, why would they be stealing the count's daughter? As he fell asleep, he heard the dogs returning to camp, burrowing into the snowbanks where they would curl up in a ball and sleep, the warmth of their breath heating the air of their small snow cocoons.

Well before light, they were up and Fargo found the count pacing by the fire. He told him he'd like a word and they moved away out of earshot. Fargo told the count what he'd overheard, leaving out the fact that he'd spied on the count too.

Count Victoroff looked worried.

"This is strange indeed," he said. "Maybe you did not hear words right."

"No," Fargo said. "I heard right."

"Impossible," the count said. "This Bull Slade is very reliable. Tough and good. Maybe he means someone else. I have hired him to . . . to save my daughter. Still, I am glad you have told me this. I will be on my guard."

The count moved away and Fargo looked after him, puzzled. If he were the count, he'd be a hell of a lot more worried than that.

By dawn they were on the trail again. This time, some of the other men tramped the trail in front of the sleds. Despite the cold, Fargo knew the river was still too dangerous. So, they made their way slowly. Sixty, in his swallowtail snowshoes, strode beside the sled while Fargo drove the dog team. The dogs were still tired and sore from their plunge in the icy water the day before and he was just as glad they weren't running full out. There was no opportunity to tell Sixty what he'd over-heard the night before.

All around them, the hills were clad in black forest and white snow, endless miles of empty wilderness. Fargo's sharp eyes scouring the brush caught the occasional leap of a hare or a ptarmi-gan, both in winter white. Once, as they rounded the edge of a meadow, he spotted the tail end of antelope disappearing at the far side, and another time, the low swift-moving shape of wolves run-ning through the trees. The dogs raised a ruckus when they caught the odor and they began to veer off the trail, then balk and turn so that the traces got hopelessly tangled and the sleds had to be called to a halt until the dogs could be quieted and set right again.

At noon, Fargo ventured out onto the river again. He walked well away from the watery ice near the shoreline toward the center of the wide Yukon. Here, the ice was ridged and bumpy. It was thicker than the ice from the day before. He knelt and brushed back the snow, then heard footsteps nearing. He glanced up to see Count Victoroff.

"What do you think of ice today, Mr. Fargo?" the count asked pleasantly. "Is better?"

"There's all kinds of ice," Fargo said, resting back on his heels and looking across the wide icy expanse. "There's star ice—real hard and clear. There's mush ice. There's anchor ice. A man's got to know what kind of ice he's looking at."

"Incredible," the count said. "Where did you learn all this?" Fargo opened his mouth to speak the name of his old friend Pete, then thought better of it.

"Any man who's been up and down this river once or twice gets to know ice," Fargo said, standing. "It is thicker today. We're farther upriver now and after that cold snap last night, I think we'll risk it." His eyes swept across the gray expanse of the low scudding clouds. "It's not going to get warmer anytime soon."

Count Victoroff laughed and clapped him on the back as they headed back toward shore where the sleds waited in a line. Fargo thought of his conversation with the count about Slade. Maybe the man was just hopelessly stupid.

"Mush!" Fargo shouted. Long-Tooth looked back at Fargo for a moment, as if questioning his sanity, then stepped gingerly out onto the river ice. The team followed and the sled skidded down the embankment and slid across the ice. Fargo flicked the whip unnecessarily above the dogs' heads as they pulled the sled out toward the middle ice— not too close to shore where the shallow water, warmed by each day's sun, would keep it thin, and not midstream of the big river where the ice had only just closed over the waters and might still be chancy. Fargo knelt in the sled, his eyes focused on the white expanse before them, looking for any sign of darkness, any break in the snow which would indicate thinner ice below.

Sixty crawled forward on the sled and re-arranged the packs so he could sit close and help keep watch. A few times, rounding a huge curve of the mighty river, Fargo slowed the dogs to a bare walk as he and Sixty consulted about the river currents, measuring the rocks and the inclination of the surrounding hills, reading where the river would be deepest, where the sun would shine each day and where the ice would be thickest. Once they had to skirt on rim ice around a dark patch where the ice hadn't yet closed up and the sled dogs looked nervously over at the open water.

Through the long afternoon, under the white sky, the dogs made excellent time. The ice was hard and fast with just enough snow for the dogs to grip. The sleds ran on, a string of men and dogs through the white silence. Fargo and Sixty pulled out far ahead, scouting the best ice and the smoothest route up the broad river. By later afternoon, as darkness was falling, they had pulled a good mile in front of the rest. Fargo reined in the dogs, turned about and told Sixty what he'd overheard in the forest the night before. Sixty's face grew grave as he listened.

"Hell, you figured right, Fargo," the old man muttered. "That mangy Bull Slade is up to no good. That's clear to me. Thing is, what's it all about?" Sixty's lined face screwed up thoughtfully. "What's the big secret about rescuing the count's daughter?"

"Damned if I know," Fargo said. "But they plan to kill us too once we've found the girl." Fargo gazed across the ice at the approaching sleds and then his eyes traveled upriver to a spot on the far bank, barely visible in the lowering dusk. "There's Anvik," he said, pointing toward the small Ingalik Indian village, barely visible, where they would stop for the night. "If you want," Fargo said lightly, "you can stay there while I take this bunch on up-river."

"Stay in Anvik? The hell you say!" Sixty sputtered, shaking his beard, his blue eyes flashing. "What the hell you thinking of, Trailsman? And what're you doing pointing out that town to me like I never been there before? You think you can drag me into this mess and then stay in it alone? Why I gotta stick around so you don't get in any trouble!"

"All right, all right!" Fargo said with a laugh.

"You think for one minute Old Sixty would give up the chance to maybe get some revenge on the skunks that did in Petey-boy?" the old man started in again. "What do you take me for? Some lily-livered southlander with perfume in his veins?"

Fargo smiled to himself. Well, fine. He'd be glad for Sixty's company. But he'd wanted to offer the old man a chance to get out now while the getting was good. The odds weren't great. Two of them against Bull Slade and his nasty gang. And there was no telling what would happen once they got far into the back country. The other sleds were coming into shouting distance.

"Anvik! Anvik!" Fargo called out to them, pointing to the distant village. He started the dogs up again, pulling out across the wide expanse of the Yukon, heading toward the village. Behind him, Sixty was still outraged and muttering to himself.

Anvik huddled on the northern bank of the Yukon. On the river ice in front of the town, Fargo spotted several knots of Ingalik fishermen gathered around dark holes chopped into the ice, raising their webbed traps for the last time that day and preparing to go in for the night. The men spotted the approaching sleds and waved a greeting.

The village began to stir. Children scurried around everywhere. In the dusk, Fargo spotted the communal building in the center of town. The long house of wood and sod, half buried in the frozen earth, was frosted with blown snow. Clustered around it were kutchins, smaller dwellings half buried in the soil against the cold, each marked by a gray wisp rising through the smokehole. The small domed lodges, roofed with skins held down with branches and sticks, looked like the mounds of a prairie dog town. Elsewhere, pilings held wooden structures eight feet above ground—caches where the food was kept, frozen and safe from predators.

A crowd of Ingaliks gathered on the bank, shouting and waving in the gloom. Boys ventured out onto the ice, several of them driving dogs before them while they held on to their tails and were pulled across the ice until they fell, laughing.

"I got a good friend in Anvik," Sixty shouted. "Ingalik by the name of White-Walker. Met him through Petey-boy."

"White-Walker." Fargo spoke the name in surprise. Yes, he remembered the man—tall, quiet, and solemn. He'd met White-Walker once before on a long hunt with MacKenzie. The Ingalik was one of the best woodsmen he'd ever run across.

"Know him?" Sixty asked. Fargo nodded.

Fargo spotted a sloping bank with plenty of room for all the sleds and he brought the team in toward shore. The sled came to a halt and was quickly swarmed by boys, all dressed in colorfully embroidered fur parkas, jabbering in their native tongue. Fargo remembered the Ingaliks—their language was Athapaskan, similar to the tongues of the Apaches and Navajos. He remembered enough of it to understand the boys' chattering. Fargo and Sixty piled out and began tugging the sled up the bank. The other sleds pulled in behind them.

"Hey there," Sixty said in Athapaskan, grabbing the jacket of one small boy as he sped by. "You know White-Walker?"

The round-faced boy laughed merrily and the other boys joined in as Sixty looked around at them, confused.

"Know him?" the boy replied. "I am Sitting-Wolf. White-Walker is my father!" Sixty laughed then and held the boy at arm's length looking him up and down.

"Yep, yep," the old man said. "So old White-Walker finally got hitched up," he said to himself. "Well, Mr. Sitting-Wolf, you go tell your father that old Sixty-Mile Sam has just hit town."

The boy ran off to do his bidding. Fargo and Sixty set to unharnessing the dogs. A huge pack of Ingalik dogs, many of them almost full-blooded wolf, ran excitedly back and forth nearby. The sled dogs, sighting them, set up a frenzied howl and the Ingalik children shouted. Sixty put his hands over his ears and Fargo laughed.

"Let's feed 'em quick before they go gallivanting for the night," Sixty suggested. Fargo pulled the frozen bear meat out of the canvas bag and broke it up into portions which he threw to each dog as it was unharnessed by Sixty. In a few minutes, their dogs all fed, Fargo and Sixty hoisted a pack of belongings onto their shoulders and made toward the longhouse, trailed by the shouting children.

Halfway along, they were met by a tall, thin man hurrying toward them. His long body moved with grace and sureness. Within the fur-lined hood, his dark face was marked with a mustache and sparse chin beard. But his eyes were what held Fargo's attention. They were dark eyes like all the north people's. But these were eyes that seemed to be looking far and were as still as a pool of water on a windless day. This was White-Walker.

"Sky-Gazer!" the Ingalik said, grasping Sixty's hand. White-Walker hardly ever smiled, Fargo remembered, but it was obvious he was pleased. "Many many years." He and the old man pumped hands for a moment, then Sixty turned and gestured toward Fargo.

"You know Skye Fargo here?" At the name, White-Walker turned and nodded.

"Good tracker, good shooter," White-Walker said, shaking Fargo's hand warmly. "I remember well."

"We went hunting together with Pete MacKenzie," Fargo explained to Sixty.

"And now Petey-boy's been killed," Sixty put in. White-Walker registered no surprise.

"I have heard," he said quietly. "Bad news came upriver. Who? Who did that?"

Just then, they heard Bull Slade's and Count Victoroff's voices behind them.

"We'll talk later," Fargo said, turning about.

"So, this is village of Anvik!" the count said. He drew a deep breath of the cold air and exhaled heartily and pulled up his fur collar. "Reminds me of Siberia. Some of the old towns in the Motherland." He looked about at the tiny village and the fishermen coming in off the ice, hauling their strings of fish behind them.

"Count Victoroff, this is White-Walker," Fargo said. The Russian offered his hand and the Ingalik shook it, expressionless.

"This is the count's expedition," Sixty said to White-Walker.

"Why if it isn't old Snow-Shoe," Bull Slade said to White-Walker, slapping the Ingalik hard on the back. "Ain't seen you around for a long time. How's everything in this two-bit town?"

White-Walker nodded to Bull Slade solemnly, his body stiff. It was clear he did not like the man.

"And are you the . . . the chief of this village?" the count said, addressing White-Walker.

"The town elder is Fish-Seer," White-Walker said. He motioned for them to enter the longhouse. The dim interior was lit by two fires, one at each end. After a moment, Fargo's eyes adjusted and he saw dozens of Ingaliks clustered here and there. On one side, a row of old women sat chewing on animal pelts to soften them. Next to them, old men were chattering while they carved ritual masks and assembled fishing traps. Young women sat gossiping and stitching skins into garments with fanciful decorations and another group of men were braiding rope. Here in the longhouse, the life of the Ingalik community flourished during the cold dark winter.

White-Walker gestured for them to remove their moccasins and parkas and drape them over a pole that ran above the fire. The gear would be dry and warm when they donned them again. Then they took their seats around the fire. Fargo was relieved to see Bull Slade sit at the other fire.

An ancient man, his face crinkled with lines, sat down next to Fargo and nodded to him.

"You are the one called the Trailsman?" the old man said.

Fargo nodded.

"I am Fish-Seer," he said simply. "I have heard much talk about you from the lands to the south. My son White-Walker often talks of the time he went hunting with you and his white friend Pete MacKenzie."

At the sound of the name, Count Victoroff, sitting next to Fargo, started and looked at the old man with curiosity.

"What's he saying?" the count cut in, not understanding the native language.

"He's talking about a hunting trip," Fargo said nonchalantly.

"*Da, da*, but I hear the name of MacKenzie," Victoroff said. "Maybe . . . maybe he know something."

"MacKenzie used to come through here all the time," Fargo said. "That's all."

The count relaxed a little and sat back. The old man, not understanding English, had followed the exchange with his sharp eyes. Now he studied Fargo for a long moment.

"You are troubled, Trailsman," Fish-Seer said. "Here in Anvik we have heard the news about the death of . . . " He hesitated but did not speak MacKenzie's name again. "He was a good man and one of our village. Now I see there is trouble ahead. You are traveling with trouble. And you have questions. You are not sure of many things." Fargo nodded. The old man saw a lot more than fish. "Later, I will tell your future. But for now, tonight, you must eat. You must rest."

Fish-Seer raised his hand and motioned to some women standing nearby. They disappeared and soon returned with huge baskets of roasted pine nuts. Another woman brought a long skewer of speared meat, which she turned over the fire as it began to sizzle. She sprinkled herbs over the broiling meat and turned it.

Someone pressed a wooden bowl into his hands and Fargo noticed a young woman, lithe and pretty, her long hair caught back in loops and braided with colorful beaded threads. Above high chiseled cheeks, her black eyes glanced curiously at the strange men and she caught his gaze. She returned it, unabashed, as she circulated among them with a basket of dried antelope pemmican. When she reached him, she leaned over to offer him the basket of pemmican. As she did so, a beaded necklace she wore swung forward and the neckline of her tunic gaped. Fargo, rather than reaching for the pemmican, caught the swinging beaded necklace and held it for a moment in his palm. His eyes traveled to the gap in her clothing where he could see her small dark tipped breasts swaying.

"Pretty," he said in Athapaskan. "Very pretty."

The young woman followed the direction of his gaze and laughed, her dark eyes merry, as she offered him the basket again with a gentle nudge. Reluctantly, he released the necklace and took some pemmican and she moved on around the circle, glancing back at him over her shoulder. Fish-Seer glanced at her, then back at Fargo, and smiled.

The feast lasted for hours as course after course of meat appeared—bear, antelope, moose, deer, rabbit, oily beaver, seal and salmon. The dishes included roasted meat, boiled meat, pemmicans, herbed stews, even strips of raw meat sliced thin. There were summer berries preserved in seal oil and flat cakes made of trading post flour mixed with wild dill. Again and again, the young woman with the flashing black eyes knelt before him, offering him another delicious course. Just when Fargo thought the meal was at last over, another dish would appear.

Meanwhile, the talk ranged from the scarcity of game in the upper Yukon this season to stories of surviving the treacherous winters. Sixty told a tale of polar bear hunting with the Aleuts farther north and how one day they had come on a camp with three dead white men—tenderfeet—who had killed their first polar bear and eaten the liver, not knowing it was poison. The count told stories of his estate in the Ukraine, of boar hunts in his forest and the serfs in their tunics out in the wheat fields.

"You . . . own these . . . serfs?" White-Walker said. It was the first time he had spoken all evening.

"*Nyet, nyet,*" Count Victoroff replied. "The serfs belong to the land. It is the law of my country. The Tsar decreed it."

"So, you own these men," White-Water persisted, trying to understand.

"Only the land," the count said impatiently. "I own the land."

"But the men must do what you say," White-Walker persisted.

"*Da, da,*" the count said. "But I am a boyar and they are mere serfs. That is the way it is. It's always been that way in my country."

Someone asked about the winters in the Ukraine and as the talk went on, Fargo noticed that White-Walker sat back with a thoughtful look on his face and did not speak again.

Finally, the women brought hot honey tea and Fargo knew the feast was finally over. Fish-Seer patted his hand.

"Now I will tell the future," he said. The men around the fire fell silent.

"Oh, the fortune-telling," Count Victoroff muttered.

Fish-Seer gestured and the pretty dark-eyed woman brought over a large basket and placed it beside the old man. Inside lay a collection of bones. Fish-Seer slowly raised one after the other and Fargo recognized the shoulder bones of antelope, bear, moose, beaver, wolf. Fish-Seer looked several times at Fargo and then chose a large bone from the shoulder of a bear. The young woman passed him two long sticks and the old man held the bone balanced on them in the middle of the roaring flames. The sticks began burning and the bone quickly blackened, then cracked in several places. After a time, the old man removed the bone from the fire and placed it on the ground in front of him. He bent over the smoking hulk.

"There is much danger on the trail ahead," the old man said slowly. "I see many men fighting." He glanced at Fargo. "I see that the men you are leading will win this fight."

"Well, that *is* good news," Count Victoroff said heartily. "What else?"

"I see death too," Fish-Seer said. The old man's eyes widened and he fell silent.

"Whose death?" the count asked, his voice nervous in the tense silence.

Fish-Seer shook his head, rose, and gathered his blanket around him. He started to move off, then stopped and spoke, as if to himself, "The future cannot be changed. The bones have spoken."

The men, their mood spoiled by Fish-Seer's somber words, got up slowly and left the long-house. Fargo sat looking at the charred bear bone before him. Only Sixty and White-Walker sat silently beside him. The fire died down to embers.

"I will come with you," White-Walker said suddenly. "I do not believe my father's words. I believe that the future can be changed." Fargo looked at the strong man with the clear silent eyes.

"You don't know what you're getting into," Fargo said to White-Walker. Then he and Sixty told the Ingalik all that had happened, from their meeting in Vancouver to the conversation overheard the day before.

"Without my help, you will die," White-Walker said. "That is clear to me. I will be ready to come tomorrow."

The three of them sat for a while in silence. Then Fargo heard a rustle at the door. It was the dark-eyed woman. Fargo smiled and she smiled back. White-Walker looked from one to the other.

"You like my cousin?" he asked Fargo, nudging him in the ribs. "Her name is Water-Song and she sleeps alone tonight." Fargo rose and made his way to her. Behind him, he heard Sixty's voice.

"There used to be a widow named Red-Feather. She still around?" Fargo heard White-Walker laugh and then he lost the rest as Water-Song took his arm and led him out into the night. He grabbed his parka, moccasins, and pack as he passed by and donned them as they exited. He found himself out in the blowing bitter cold as she led him the short distance toward one of the small kutchins where the embers from a fire rose into the night sky. Despite the cold, he paused a moment and drew her toward him, wrapping his arms around her.

Above them the magical mysterious northern lights were playing across the starry sky. The weird colors seemed to drip down the sky and then flicker prismatically, blue, green, rose, and purple. He nuzzled her hair, inhaling the sweet fragrance of her.

"Those are the spirits dancing in the sky," Water-Song said with a laugh. "That is good fortune." Then she turned and pulled him into the kutchin.

The small interior was fire-warmed, bathed in the light of the flickering flames, and carpeted with thick furs. Fargo pulled off his moccasins and parka. Water-Song took the jacket from him and as it fell open she gasped.

"Oh! My Red Bear!" He turned to see her touching the painted picture inside his parka of the bear face. "This is good luck again," she said. "I made this parka." Fargo laughed and pulled her toward him.

"And I bought it down in Alakanuk," he said. "So, I like it even better knowing that you made it. You have many talents."

Water-Song pushed him away teasingly as she slowly began undoing her hair.

"You do not know what talents I have, Trailsman," she said. "But tonight, I will show you."

4

Water-Song looked up at him, her eyes shining, as she slowly unbraided the colored beaded ornaments from her hair and let it fall around her, a dark shining mass of blackness which gleamed as darkly as her eyes and fell below her hips. Fargo, kneeling on the furs in the low-roofed kutchin, moved toward her, but she giggled and pushed him away as she slowly pulled off her moccasins and the long leggings beneath her skirt. He glimpsed her curved and tawny legs. Her hair fell around her shoulders and over her, as she undid the fastenings of her antelope skin dress and let it fall away from her. She was naked, but covered by her long dark hair. She glanced up at him and slowly, very slowly, parted the hair so that he could see her high-mounded breasts, dark nippled.

Then, suddenly, she lay back and he saw her slender waist, the generous curve of her hips, her rounded legs, smooth and supple, and her satiny skin gleaming in the firelight. She smiled and parted her legs slightly and moisture glinted among the dark tangle of fur. She held out her arms to him and Fargo sank down on top of her, his mouth covering hers, drinking in the unfamiliar sweetness of her, his hands exploring the smooth arc of her ribs, the comforting fullness of her soft breasts.

He slid his tongue into her mouth and she pulled, drank him in deeper, hungrily, as her hands fumbled at his belt, undoing it, then finding the buttons on his jeans, until at last he felt her hand reaching for him and finding him, huge and rock hard.

"Ah," she breathed, stroking his shaft and circling the velvet tip with one tentative finger. She shuddered as he moved his hand downward, finding her bush, her wetness, the folded lips, the hard knot of her desire which he teased, rubbing gently as she writhed on the furs, moaning. Her hips began a low rhythmic thrusting against his hand. He stripped off his jeans and shirt as she raised her knees and he lowered himself onto her, sinking down into her warmth and softness, sliding into her small, tight sheath. She brought up her ankles and placed them on his shoulders, opening fully to him as he pushed into her, feeling her narrowness around his throbbing shaft. As he pushed into her again and again, he rotated his hips, rubbing up against her folded lips each time and she moaned, thrusting upward to meet him.

"Yes, yes," she said, tossing her head from side to side, her long black hair gleaming in the firelight. He could feel the gathering at the base, swelling. He slowed, not wanting to finish.

Water-Song smiled up at him and pulled her legs from his shoulders, then firmly pushed him aside. He rolled away from her and lay on the skins, his throbbing, glistening shaft full and hard.

74

She knelt beside him and suddenly took him into her mouth. The sensation was indescribable. Her tongue flickered and sucked and pulled him to the very edge and just as he was about to lose control, she would slow, and then begin again. Again and again, she teased him to near explosion and then brought him back again. Fargo had never felt anything like it. After a while, he reached over and stroked her thigh, then tickled upward toward her wetness and found the folded lips, the tight portal.

She murmured and suddenly, he pulled her toward him, covering her with his mouth, holding her lips apart and seeking the tight, hard button of her with the tip of his tongue and flicking it, sucking it again and again.

"Ah! Ah!" she screamed. He sucked harder, his fingers in her, pulsing back and forth, his mouth tasting her salty sweet musk. He was hot in her mouth now, huge and pounding, unable to hold back, the explosion gathered and began, slowly, firing upward, a fountain of fire as he felt her tighten beneath his tongue and vibrate inside and he came, shudderingly, pouring out into her as she trembled violently and shivered once, twice, and again, crying out.

"Ah, yes! Yes!" she moaned and writhed.

It was over. Fargo lay back, resting his head on her thigh. He looked down and she was smiling, eyes half closed as she lay nestling against his legs. Exhausted, he closed his eyes, listened to the crackle of the fire, and thought of Fish-Seer's words.

*   *   *

The next morning Fargo emerged from the kutchin to find trouble brewing. A group of the count's men and villagers were gathered. Hearing angry voices, Fargo hurried forward pushing toward the center of the crowd.

"And I say we need the extra sled and the extra man!" Sixty was shouting at Bull Slade. White-Walker stood to the side, watching silently. Sixty spotted Fargo and turned to him. "You'll back me on this, won't you, Fargo? White-Walker says he's willing to come along with us, bring his own supplies which would replace the ones we lost in the Yukon, thanks to you, Slade." Bull Slade growled at the old man. "White-Walker said he'd help out for no pay. Hell, we could use a man like him, knows that country even better'n you or me. Slade here says he can't come. Whatddya you think?"

"The more the merrier," Fargo said coolly. "I say he comes."

"And I say he doesn't," Bull Slade growled. "And I'm the one leading this here expedition. You've crossed me one too many times, Fargo." Slade took a menacing step forward, his hand on the hilt of the long knife at his belt.

"What is going on here?" Count Victoroff shouted, pushing his way through to them. "What? You two at it again?"

"I just gave my opinion," Fargo said. "White-Walker offered to come along and help us out. For free. I said sure. We lost that sled full of supplies and two men. If you want your daughter back, you take help wherever you can find it." Count Victoroff glanced at the silent Ingalik curiously.

"Why do you want to come with us?" he asked suspiciously.

"I hear these men you are going to kill are the ones killed Pete MacKenzie," White-Walker said, his eyes steady.

"MacKenzie . . . *da, da,* that is right," Victoroff said hastily. "MacKenzie found out where they were hiding and came back to Alakanuk. They tracked him down there and killed him. They still have my daughter." The count looked at White-Walker for a moment. "But what about this MacKenzie?"

"Three times he saved my life," White-Walker said. "So, I would go with you to find men who killed MacKenzie. And I will take their lives in return."

Count Victoroff stood thinking for a long moment.

"He'll bring his own supplies and sled," Sixty put in.

"You're not considering this!" Bull Slade sputtered.

"Why not?" the count said, glancing at him.

"Because . . . " Slade gave up and stomped off. Fargo knew exactly what Bull meant. When it came time to get rid of Fargo and Sixty and the count, Bull Slade would have White-Walker on their hands too.

"He's damn good on the trail," Fargo said.

"*Da, da,* said Victoroff at last. "This White-Walker can come and help kill killers of MacKenzie. And rescue Natasha. Why not?" Victoroff turned and pushed his way out of the crowd. Sixty winked at Fargo, who breathed a sign of relief.

Well, so now there were three of them against eighteen. The crowd broke up slowly and Sixty stood talking to White-Walker. Fargo spotted Fish-Seer standing at the door of a kutchin, with his hand on the shoulder of his grandson, Sitting-Wolf. The boy was tugging on the old man's hand, but Fish-Seer shook his head and retreated into the lodge. The boy bounded over to his father, then stood silently by until he and Sixty had finished speaking.

"What is it, my son?" White-Walker asked.

"Can I come with you, Father?"

"This is not a hunt for meat," White-Walker said, shaking his head.

For the next few hours, they busied themselves readying the sleds and rounding up the dog teams, which were running wild with the Ingalik pack. White-Walker loaded his sled, which was compact and low to the ground, designed for speed but able to pack enough for two men to make a very long journey. After much bustling and bartering with the Ingaliks, and just as the sun was coming up far to the southeast, the expedition was ready to depart and the reluctant dogs were put back in their traces. Fargo broke the ice from their runners with the gee pole and cast an eye over the sled. It looked fuller than before but he didn't stop to wonder at it. Sixty was going to take the first lap riding with White-Walker so that they could catch up on old times.

A crowd gathered on the shore to see them off. Fargo looked in vain for the shining dark head of Water-Song. He was disappointed not to see her there. Well, sometimes women were like that, he thought.

Fargo cried "Mush" and ran alongside the sled as the dogs tugged it down the slope toward the frozen Yukon. It gathered speed as it hit the ice and Fargo jumped aboard. The dogs had had a good night's rest and Fargo hoped with Sixty riding on the other sled, they'd have an easy day's run of it. The rest of the sleds fell into line behind him and they were off, running fast up the frozen river, heading north-northeast up the wide Yukon. It was a clear, cold day with a stiff wind blowing from the west. All day long, they ran hard over the frozen river, with only a short break at midday to feed and water the dogs.

Fargo's team wasn't running as well as he'd expected, given the lightness of the load. The dogs were pulling as hard as if Sixty had been aboard and, watching them, Fargo wondered several times if the dunking in the cold waters of the Yukon was still having an effect on the team.

As the light faded, they found themselves almost fifty miles upriver from Anvik, a good day's run. Fargo spotted a rocky cliff that provided a shallow overhang with plenty of firewood nearby and they headed for it. They pulled the sleds up into a half circle around the base of the cliff, and a party of men went out to gather firewood, which was plentiful in the piney forest. The count left with others on a hunting foray in the long, slow dusk.

Sixty was unharnessing the dogs as Fargo went to scrounge up some meat for their dinner. He unlashed the canvas cover from atop the pile of supplies on the sled and threw back the tarp. There, huddled in a thick fur, was Water-Song.

"What the hell?" Fargo said. Sixty came running and when he caught sight of the woman, he laughed with glee.

"Oh, Fargo, she's sweet on you," Sixty said.

The uproar drew the attention of several of the men, who gathered nearby. Fargo took one of Water-Song's hands and pulled her out of the sled.

"Hey, nice load of supplies, Trailsman," one of the men shouted.

"How 'bout passing her around?" another called out.

"Yeah, I'd like a piece of her ass," another said.

Water-Song didn't understand English and she laughed happily at Fargo's surprise. Hell, this complicated things, he thought. This would be a dangerous trip and she couldn't come along. It was impossible. Not with the bloodbath that was sure to happen at the end of the trail. But how would they get her the fifty miles back to Anvik? White-Walker caught sight of her and hurried over.

"What are you doing here?" he asked her angrily in Athapaskan. Water-Song hung her head.

"It was because of the red bear," she said quietly.

Infuriated, White-Walker raised his hand to strike her, but Fargo held him back.

"No, wait," he said.

"I sewed the red bear into the jacket and Fish-Seer helped me to make a spell to bring me a man," Water-Song explained. "And the red bear came back to me. *He* is wearing it."

White-Walker glanced at Fargo for an explanation and Fargo showed him the bear's face inside the parka. Instead of being angry, White-Walker looked amazed.

"This is powerful medicine," he said. He glanced at Water-Song again. "Fish-Seer taught you this?" She nodded her head. "Then she must go where she goes," White-Walker said. "It is the way of the spirits. We cannot fight them." He walked away but Fargo could tell he was troubled about something. Fargo watched the Ingalik head out into the forest, probably to see if he could find some game.

Meanwhile, word had spread that there was a woman stowaway in camp. The men crowded around to stare at Water-Song and Bull Slade came pushing through.

"What's all this?" He stopped short and stared at Water-Song. "This your idea, Fargo?"

"Don't ride me, Slade," Fargo said. "She's a stowaway."

"And you're a goddamn liar," Slade shot back. "You want every dirty Indian in the Yukon on this trip."

Fargo had had enough. He stepped forward and his powerful fist shot out, connecting hard on Slade's jaw. The big man's head snapped back and he reeled a few steps.

"Had enough?" Fargo said. "Now quit riding me."

Slade was undoing his parka, his eyes focused on Fargo with hatred that burned like fire.

"He wants to fight," Sixty said. Fargo slipped out of his parka as the men formed a ring, shouting encouragement to Bull Slade. Water-Song huddled close to Sixty. Now, Slade was in the ring, his hands clawing the air, his eyes red.

Fargo had barely turned about when Slade rushed him with a roar and caught him off-guard. The full force of the big man hit Fargo and he went down with Slade on top of him, punching. Fargo hit the snow and rolled over in a desperate attempt to get Slade off him. The man was a dirty fighter. With one hand, he tried to put one of Fargo's eyes out, but Fargo caught his arm and slowly, slowly wrenched it upward while Slade's face turned purple with the exertion. The crowd of men booed. Suddenly, Slade spat in his face. Rather than flinching, Fargo thrust upward with a mighty right into Slade's belly, then followed it with a rolling left around to bring Slade pitching sideways off him.

The men hissed and yelled encouragement at Slade. Fargo leapt onto Slade and pummeled him again and again with his fists. He could feel the man weakening but suddenly, he felt a blow on his back. Someone in the crowd had kicked him from behind. Pain shot through him, as well as shock.

"Hey! No fair!" Sixty yelled out.

The crowd laughed and jeered and Fargo, momentarily stunned by the blow, let up on Slade. In that brief instant, Slade heaved upward and rolled out from under him. Fargo spun about and slowly stood, crouching and facing Slade, who was just coming to his feet. Again, he felt a boot on his backside.

"I'll take you all on," Fargo growled. "But one at a time. Not like a pack of wolves."

The men laughed and someone threw Slade a knife. Water-Song cried out and Fargo heard Sixty calling out for somebody to give him a knife.

Everything became very quiet now. Fargo, his eye on Slade, leaned over and pulled the Arkansas toothpick from his ankle holster. A murmur went up as the two men silently circled one another, every muscle tense.

Slade feinted and Fargo moved in as Slade's long knife slashed, whistling through the air. Fargo ducked just in time and brought his knee into Slade's groin.

The man howled with pain and doubled over as the men shouted. Served him right, Fargo thought. Bull Slade came up again, murder in his eyes, his knife raised. Fargo had seen that look before. It was the look of a man who wouldn't be stopped until he or his opponent lay dead. Fargo knew it was now a fight to the finish.

Fargo made a sudden move left, then pulled back as Slade jumped at him, putting his foot out and catching Slade's calf. The big man went down in a sprawl, cursing. He came to his feet again, the rage hotter, his face bloodied.

"Come on, guys!" Slade spat. "Help me out here." Fargo leapt away from the edge of the crowd as a man's foot kicked forward. He heard Sixty's voice protesting, shouting over the roar of the crowd, but he only had eyes for Slade's long gleaming knife and his red eyes. He felt another blow across his back and just then, Slade rushed him. Fargo brought up his blade, but someone in the crowd pushed him again and he lost his balance, went down and felt Slade fall on top of him, crushingly, felt the cold bite of the metal blade in his shoulder.

"AEEEE!" screamed Water-Song.

Around him, Fargo heard all hell break loose as he struggled to get a grip on Slade. Suddenly, the big man's face was inches from his and he held Fargo's knife hand pinioned on the snow. Slade's own knife was poised just above Fargo's throat, wavering as Fargo struggled to hold it from descending.

His shoulder was cut bad, Fargo knew. And it was the arm that was holding Slade's knife hand. He could feel the warm blood and the deep throb of the wound. Still, he held his iron grip steady as Slade grunted with the effort. Slowly, slowly, Slade's knife descended toward Fargo's throat as Slade's sweating face grinned above him.

Just when Slade thought he'd almost won, Fargo saw his opening. He dropped his knife and wrenched his good arm free, bringing it up and around Slade's neck. Caught completely by surprise, Slade dropped his knife and thrashed about for a grip, but Fargo thrust upward and half rolled, flipped, and caught him in a grip with his face half down in the snow, arms helplessly flailing. It was over.

"What is this? What is happening here?" Count Victoroff pushed his way to the center of the ring. In a second he took in the sight of the two bloodied men and the discarded knives. "What? What?" He looked around again and caught sight of Wind-Song huddled next to Sixty. "Woman in the camp!" he said. "And there is fighting already. Who brought this woman?"

"She's a stowaway," Fargo said, getting to his feet. Slade spit in his direction, then got up, his face running blood.

"Send her back to Anvik," the count said. "This trail is no place for a woman."

"How? On which sled?" Fargo pointed out. "We need every man and every sled we've got. And the supplies are packed tight." The count cursed in Russian.

"You are right," he said.

"How about this," Fargo said. "The Russian trading post at Nulato is just upriver a couple of days. That's just before we turn off into the back country. We can leave Water-Song there for the time being."

"*Da, da,*" Victoroff said, gruffly. "But until then, I do not want any more trouble. That goes for you too, Mr. Slade."

Bull shot Fargo a resentful look and the crowd broke up slowly. Fargo stood wiping his knife against his shirt, hardly feeling the cold. He watched Bull Slade's back. Next time it would be to the death, he realized. That's how much Bull Slade had come to hate him. Sixty and Water-Song came running up.

"Let's go tend that shoulder," Sixty said, clucking his tongue.

Fargo followed them toward the fire. Of everything that had happened that afternoon, Slade's hatred had been the least of it. He'd known about that all along. What had bothered him were the shouts and jeers of the other men, the nasty kicks in his back. He realized that the five of them—Sixty, White-Walker, the count, Water-Song, and himself—were very much alone. The men in the expedition—Slade's men—were ranged against them like a pack of slavering wolves and he realized that from here on out, he couldn't afford to drop his guard for a second.

"Let's put up our camp on one side," Sixty said sullenly. "I don't feel like bedding down next to any of those fellows tonight."

"Suits me," Fargo said. They took a spot at one end of the overhanging cliff, where the rocks sheltered them from the wind and the blowing snow. Deep beneath the overhang, tufts of yellow grass showed.

Sixty pulled the pile of fuel he gathered earlier into a heap and lit a fire, starting with dry moss and twigs and then feeding it with limbs, then logs. Soon a roaring campfire was blazing. He left to gather more wood for the night while Water-Song placed large rocks around the fire for cooking. She boiled water in a tin pot and removed Fargo's shirt, daubing at the bloodied flesh. She pulled a pouch from her skirts and sprinkled herbs into the water, then daubed again. Sixty pulled out a bottle of iodine which Fargo himself poured into the wound. It hurt like hell but it would keep the infection away. The knife had gone deep but hadn't sliced any of the muscles seriously. His hand was still working. Then Water-Song pulled a small leather packet from the bag of her things on the sled. She began threading a needle.

"You going to stitch this?" he asked.

"I sew your coat," Water-Song said. "Now I sew your shoulder." Fargo laughed and watched with admiration as she bent over his shoulder. Biting her lip with concentration, her brow furrowed with worry for him, she pierced his flesh with the needle and soon had stitched the wound shut. She daubed more of the iodine on the surface, then tore up an old shirt of Fargo's to bandage the shoulder.

"Neat job," Fargo said, when it was done. He had had a lot of doctors bandage him over the years and no one had done it better than this Ingalik woman.

"Fish-Seer taught me medicine and many other things," Water-Song said modestly. Fargo realized that, for all her impulsiveness in stowing away on his sled, she was a levelheaded woman. And, if he understood right, even her stowing away hadn't been so impulsive. She had sewn the painted bear inside his jacket in order to bring herself a man. And, damn it, he'd come along. Fargo stroked his chin as he watched her move around the fire, putting everything in order. Trouble was, he wasn't the settling kind. Water-Song was just the kind of woman who wouldn't understand that. Well, he'd worry about that later.

White-Walker returned with a brace of rabbits and four fat squirrels. When he saw Fargo's bandaged shoulder and the separate fire, there were questions in his eyes.

Sixty filled him in while the four of them set to cleaning the game, spearing the meat on sticks and roasting it over the flames. Around the other fire, the men were laughing. When they had eaten and the cold wind was whistling past, Fargo suddenly looked about.

"The dogs didn't go out tonight," he remarked.

The four of them looked over to where a few of the dogs could be seen digging into the snowbank. Fargo remembered earlier having seen them skulking about camp, but he had thought nothing of it.

"Big wolf pack nearby," White-Walker said grimly. "Not much game out there."

"But you found some," Sixty said, patting his belly and burping contentedly.

"White-Walker is smarter than wolves," Water-Song said proudly. For a brief instant, White-Walker smiled at her.

"Fix the places to sleep," he told her sternly. "While we talk man talk." Water-Song got up from the fire and went over to the sled, unrolling the canvas and busying herself with preparations for sleep.

"We will leave her at the Russian trading post," Fargo said, "where she'll be safe. None of us is safe with this bunch."

Another burst of raucous laughter exploded from the direction of the other campfire.

"Don't you think that the count can keep those men under control?" Sixty said.

"For a while," Fargo mused. "But their allegiance is really to Bull Slade. He gathered 'em and hired 'em. And he's the one who's telling 'em what to do."

"And one of these days he's going to tell 'em to string the rest of us up," Sixty put in. "And the count's as trusting as an unmilked cow."

"Looks like it," Fargo said. "I just hope we can find out what the hell this is all about before that time comes."

"Yep," Sixty muttered. "What I can't figure out—"

Just then a chorus of howls broke out from the forest nearby, yips and the long drawn-out moans of wolves. There was silence from the other campfire as the men listened.

"They are close in tonight," White-Walker said.

Fargo heard a whine and Long Tongue came up, wagging his tail and looked anxiously behind him into the woods. Fargo wrapped his arm around the wolf dog's thick ruff. The dog nuzzled him for a moment, then turned and walked off again toward the snowbank to dig a sleeping place.

"Even the dogs are nervous," Sixty remarked. "Must be a big pack."

"Seventy wolves," White-Walker said. "Maybe more. I saw their tracks."

Fargo whistled. Usually packs were no more than fifteen, maybe two dozen. More than that and they couldn't run down enough game to feed themselves and so would break off into smaller hunting groups.

"Let's turn in," Fargo said, rising.

Sixty built up the fire and put extra logs nearby so he could stoke it again in the middle of the night. Nothing like a fire to keep wolves at bay, though they'd have to be desperate and starving to rush a camp.

Water-Song had arranged their sleeping places with a canvas tent for Sixty and another for herself and Fargo. White-Walker preferred to roll himself in blankets underneath the cliff, where the radiant heat of the fire would warm him. Fargo crawled under the canvas on top of the furs

Water-Song had carefully spread. It felt as soft as a mattress. He turned back the furs and groped underneath. She had piled spruce boughs to provide a springy bed.

"Very nice," he said. He pulled off his parka and leggings and lay down, gathering her in toward him and snuggling down beneath the furs. It was too cold to move about much, but as he lay with her warm and fragrant next to him, curled up within the larger curve of his body, he felt himself thinking of the night before and he felt himself harden. She felt it too and moved her hips suggestively against him. He kissed her hair and her neck and she reached down to pull up her tunic. He ran his hand along her satiny flank and then made love again to her, slowly and gently. As they fell asleep, Fargo listened to the wolves nearby—singing, quarreling.

In his dream the pack of wolves were all around him, red-eyed and slavering. He whirled about and saw one creeping by dragging something. Then he saw that the wolf was pulling Water-Song by the hair, away into the forest. Fargo reached for his rifle but it had turned into a gee pole. Water-Song called out to him.

No, it was real. Water-Song was calling him.

"Fargo," she said.

He was awake in an instant, awake to the sound of something moving around outside, the sound of something not right. In an instant, he was dressed, with his rifle in hand and silently exited the tent. He stood up in the freezing darkness. The other campfire had died out entirely, although their own still flickered and glowed red. Fargo glanced beyond it toward the cliff. The dark figure of White-Walker stood there beside his sleeping place, also listening to the night. There was the sound again. Gnawing. Then he saw it near the other sleds. The dark figure of a wolf. And there were a dozen of them, silent and swarming around the sleeping camp. He watched in the starlight as a wolf silently bit through the leather tethers binding the bags of meat on a sled and then, as it came loose, silently pulled the bag of meat, dragging it, slowly, slowly, with a soft hiss over the frozen ground. In the darkness, it was impossible to see what was happening to the sleds on the far side, but Fargo imagined the wolves were swarming over them too.

Fargo glanced over at White-Walker and they raised their rifles simultaneously. The four explosions of gunfire were followed by the death shriek of one wolf and the sharp cry of three others that were wounded. Instantly, the black forms turned tail and fled into the woods. The camp became a cacophony of sled dogs bursting out of their snowbanks and howling, and men staggering out of their blankets shouting, rifles in hand. In a second, Fargo and White-Walker reloaded and fired again, four shots more after the retreating wolves, and one more howl told them that at least one bullet had found its mark.

Because their sleds had been so close in near the fire with Fargo and Sixty sleeping next to them, the wolves hadn't come near. But the other men had left their sleds well away from the fire and slept under the cliff. Fargo and White-Walker walked over to survey the damage. The wolves had made off with a lot by gnawing through the tethers on the sleds and pulling off the bundles of frozen meat, more often than not, stored on top of the load. And they had robbed the camp silently and even the dogs hadn't smelled them because the wind had shifted and was blowing in toward the cliff. They were damn wily critters, Fargo thought.

The men, grumpy with sleepiness, piled the remaining supplies back on their sleds and pulled the sleds in tighter toward the cliff. They built up the fire again. Fargo spotted the count walking among the sleds, taking stock. He spotted them and hurried over.

"Such wolves!" he said, beating his hands against his sides to keep warm. "Worse than Siberia. Will they come again tonight?"

"I don't think so," Fargo said. "That meat will take the edge off their hunger.

From a distance, came the sounds of snarls and a yelp, cut off.

"And the pack will eat the three we wounded," Fargo said. "And tomorrow, they'll come back for this one we killed. That's the law of the north land."

"It is hard land," the count said. "Yes, it is like Russia. Only the strong survive. The weak must be crushed." He returned to the camp and Fargo and White-Walker walked back toward the campfire, which Sixty had built up again to a blaze. Fargo returned to the sleeping place, lost in thought. The weak must be crushed, the count had said. Not they *will* be, but they *must* be.

As he lay on the furs, his arm around Water-Song, who had fallen asleep again, Fargo thought of Fish-Seer's prediction over the charred bear bone. He had seen death and hardship. That was certain. And he had said that the men Fargo was leading would prevail. Fargo turned onto his side and banished the thoughts from his mind. He didn't believe in fortune-telling anyway.

Water-Song had fixed the fire and breakfast by the time he awoke. Fargo tested his shoulder in the morning and found that Water-Song's bandage and stitching had done well. It was sore, but healing fast. They ate quickly and called the dogs to the traces. The other camp was slow in stirring and so they waited by the fire while the other dog teams were assembled.

The day's run was much like the one the day before. The runners skimmed fast over the Yukon River ice and the mountains, hills, and valleys sped by. Fargo, kneeling in the sled with the wind against his face, was thankful for the time of silence when he could just think about all that had happened, turning over in his mind again and again Bull Slade's words, what the count had said about Natasha, about the gang of kidnappers, trying to figure out why he felt so certain that something still didn't add up.

That night they camped in the deserted buildings of an abandoned fishing camp, enjoying the luxury of a roof over their heads. The four of them shared a small cabin and the other men divided up among the other three buildings. Even though the wind whistled through cracks in the walls, the stove was kept burning all night and they slept warmly. They left early for the long run into Nulato, the Russian trading post. Bull Slade had been careful to stay out of Fargo's way since their fistfight. But Fargo was sure they'd tangle again. By the time the light faded, Nulato came into view, a ragtag collection of dark wood shacks on the bank of the frozen river. This time as they approached there was no welcoming party of women and children, but only a few of the trappers loading furs onto a sled for the trip downriver for trading at Alakanuk. They looked up, spotted the approaching caravan, and then continued their work.

Fargo steered the dogs up toward the bank and came to a halt beside the large wooden trading post in the center of the settlement. Fargo leapt out, followed by Sixty. The other sleds pulled in behind them and within a short time, the caravan's sled dogs had been unharnessed, fed, and were running in a pack up the hillside, pursued by the yipping pack of the trading post dogs. Fargo pulled the roll of frozen bearskin off the sled and headed into the post.

The interior of the wooden structure was warm and smelled of boiled potatoes, tobacco, sweat, and the fragrance of cured skins. The walls and ceiling were covered with shelves full of woven Indian blankets, folded parkas and leggings, piles of pelts, stacks of rawhide-strung snowshoes, baskets, canteens, pottery, looped harnesses, canisters of grease, canned provisions and bags of flour, sugar, beans, and cornmeal. Half a dozen men lounged around a potbellied stove. A counter ran across the back of the trading post and on it, an ornate four-legged metal pot hissed over a small yellow flame.

"Why, they've got their tea brewing in a samovar," Sixty muttered with a chuckle. "Now we know for sure they're Russians."

Behind the counter, a portly man wearing a brown-belted tunic shirt spotted them. His eyes lit up.

"Hey! You strangers! Want to buy? Sell? Make good prices!" he said in a thick accent.

Fargo and Sixty sauntered over to the counter and Fargo threw down the roll of bearskin. The trader bent over it as if sniffing it.

"Fresh skin," he said. He tugged at the edge of it, but the rolled skin was still frozen and couldn't be unrolled. "Have to wait until it's warm. Looks big. You kill this bear?" he said to Fargo. Fargo nodded. "Good size. Big grizzly. You get me more of these, I will buy them always. You got me more? Maybe outside?"

"Sorry," Fargo said. "Just this one. And we're looking for meat. Any kind, frozen for the dogs."

"I am Maxim," he said. "Trader of the Yukon. And who are you, please?"

"This here's Skye Fargo," Sixty cut in. "Everybody calls him the Trailsman. And folks call me Sixty-Mile Sam." Maxim's eyes widened and he looked from one to the other.

"I have heard many stories of both of you," he said. "But what is bringing the famous Trailsman so far from the south?"

"Trying to find a missing woman," Fargo said. Maxim's eyebrows went up and his eyes sparkled.

"Not enough women up here," he said. "This

woman, she is Russian?" Sixty nodded and Maxim's smile broadened. "You will tell me if you find her maybe? Maybe she is interested in husband? Rich trader husband with many furs? Nice husband. No beat her. You will tell her about Maxim maybe?"

"Sure," Fargo said with a chuckle.

Behind him, he heard the door open as the rest of the men came inside the trading post. He heard Bull Slade's voice and then the count's voice speaking in Russian to the group of men by the stove.

"Who is that, please?" Maxim asked, pointing.

"That's Count Victoroff," Fargo said, his eyes on the tall fur-coated figure of the count. "His daughter got kidnapped. The gang's somewhere up in the back country north of here. We're hired to help get her back. Have you heard anything about that gang? Or about the girl?"

Fargo turned back toward Maxim and saw the look of outrage on the trader's face. Slowly his face became redder and redder as if he were about to explode.

"Victoroff!" he sputtered, followed by a stream of Russian words that could only have been curses. The trader angrily pushed the bearskin across the counter toward Fargo. "Get out!" he screamed. He hastened around the counter toward where the count stood talking in Russian to the group of men by the stove.

Maxim began shouting at the men in Russian. The only word Fargo could understand was Victoroff. The reaction was immediate. The men jumped to their feet and several of them drew their knives and others grabbed for their rifles leaning against the wall. They moved forward menacingly. Bull Slade saw what was happening and shouted to his men to protect the count. The men, spread out around the room examining the goods, drew their weapons immediately and moved in around the count. In a moment, the count's men were arrayed in a half circle around Maxim and the Russian men. The Russian trappers were outnumbered, but nevertheless, Maxim cocked the rifle someone had handed him.

"Wait a minute!" Fargo shouted. "Hold on. What's this all about?"

"Get out of my trading post," Maxim said.

"No!" Fargo said. "I want an explanation."

"You. Get out," Maxim said again. He raised the rifle and aimed it right at a point between Fargo's eyes. "No talk. Get out." Fargo hesitated a moment but Maxim tightened his finger on the trigger and his eyes blazed fury.

"Let's go," Bull Slade said. The count backed out the door, surrounded by Bull Slade and his men. Fargo and Sixty reluctantly left the trading post. Just as they exited, Maxim spit after them. Fargo thought of the reaction of the owner of the general store back in Alakanuk when he had discovered they were working for Count Victoroff.

"What the hell's going on?" Sixty whispered as they retreated toward their sleds.

"Damned if I know," Fargo said. "And we can't get close enough to them to find out."

The Russians poured out the trading post door behind them, rifles still raised. The other trappers left their sleds and hurried over and, after a hasty exchange, they too grabbed their rifles. All the Russians stood in a line across the front of the trading post.

"What's this all about?" Fargo said,

"We'll camp upriver for the night," the count said angrily.

"You're not answering my question," Fargo persisted.

Count Victoroff stared at him, his eyes blazing with something that Fargo could not exactly identify.

"Politics," the count said at last. "It is politics. There are anarchists in my country. Idiots who do not want a government, they do not want order. It is Russian politics, Mr. Fargo. You would not understand."

Fargo opened his mouth to protest, but the count turned away hastily and gave orders for the men to round up the dogs. Once more, Fargo attempted to approach Maxim for an explanation, but the Russians threatened him with their rifles as he approached the post. It was some time before they could entice the dogs back into their traces and by then it was nearly dark. All that time, the Russians had not moved from their place. Dispirited and tired, the caravan made ready to go. Fargo and Sixty started up the dogs and pulled out onto the ice again in the near darkness, moving slowly as the night wind blew hard icy granules against their faces. They made camp a few miles upriver in a spot protected by a thick stand of tall spruce.

As Fargo lay under the firs with Water-Song sleeping in his arms, he thought of Maxim and the

98

Russians at the trading post. The situation was much more difficult now, he realized. They had planned to leave Water-Song at the relative safety of the trading post while they went into the dangerous back country in pursuit of Natasha and her kidnappers. And they had also counted on being able to obtain more meat for the dogs. Now they would be heading into the hardest part of the trip with a woman and short of supplies.

And Fargo wondered again what was going on between the Russians. It seemed that none of Count Victoroff's countrymen had any sympathy for his mission to get the girl Natasha back. In fact, they were downright hostile. But why? Fargo didn't buy the count's explanation of politics. It didn't ring right. But for the life of him, he couldn't imagine just what the trouble was.

5

The next day at noon, Fargo called a brief halt so the dogs could be rested. He stood and stared for the hundredth time at Pete MacKenzie's buckskin map laid out on top of the lashed canvas of the sled. Across the leather, the berry juice markings were faint but definite. Pete had indicated that he turned off the Yukon just about ten miles upriver of Nulato. Then the wavering pale red line led north-northwest through the back country and up into the mountains. It looked like a good fifty miles—two days' travel bushwhacking. But as Fargo followed the line of MacKenzie's travels, the map was water-damaged and the dim markings faded out altogether. Somewhere up there, he'd found the camp of Natasha's kidnappers. But as soon as MacKenzie had made it back to Alakanuk to tell Bull Slade, he'd been murdered.

Had the kidnappers followed Pete back down to the coast and strung him up to keep him from talking? That was the count's story. Or had Bull Slade murdered MacKenzie? If so, why? What had MacKenzie found out that was a threat to Slade? And why wouldn't Victoroff believe that they were all in danger from Slade? Fargo stared again at the map, wishing to hell it could talk.

He puzzled over the fact that MacKenzie's map had been damaged just at the most important part. It was almost as if somebody had dipped it in water just to keep the kidnapper's camp still secret. Fargo pondered this, searching for an answer, but nothing made sense.

White-Walker came striding through the snow, his face grave. He stopped and leaned against the sled.

"Not enough meat for dogs," he said. "And hunting is bad in the back country. My cousin Water-Song should not have come. And men are angry at something." His troubled eyes traveled to the scurrying forms of the other men some distance away hacking through the river ice to get water for the dogs.

"Yeah," Fargo said. It was a lot of words for the normally laconic White-Walker to speak all at once.

"Why did his tribe not help the big chief?" White-Walker continued, nodding toward Count Victoroff.

"I don't know," Fargo said. "And they're all ranged against us. You, me, and Sixty against the whole pack of Slade's men. As soon as we find the girl, they're going to try to kill us."

White-Walker nodded thoughtfully.

"Water-Song must go back to Anvik," he said shortly. "The old man can take her. They will both be out of danger. I will stay with you. Sixty must do this." Sixty, passing by on his way to harness the dogs, heard his name and stopped.

"Do what?" he asked White-Walker pleasantly.

"Take Water-Song back to Anvik where she will be safe," White-Walker said.

"And leave you and Fargo in the lurch?" Sixty said, his blue eyes blazing. "Two of you against the twenty of them? No go. I ain't no yellow-belly. Besides, she's your cousin, White-Walker. You take her back."

"I cannot leave," White-Walker said. "Because of MacKenzie."

"Hey," Sixty put in, "I knew Petie longer than either of you. I bet you a dead grizzly this bald-headed know-nothing and his gang of greasy gophers had a hand in Petie's murder. And I gotta be in on it to the bitter end! You take her back yourself."

Just then, Water-Song passed by and stopped, puzzled and curious to see them huddled together talking. White-Walker called her over.

"You have caused much trouble hiding in the sled," he admonished her in the Ingalik tongue. Her eyes filled with tears and she bit her lip. "Now one of us must take you back to Anvik, leaving the others in danger."

"Why?" she said, defiantly. "If I wish to go to Anvik, I will go. By myself. I do not need anyone to take me there."

"It's three days' travel," Sixty said dubiously. "That's dangerous for anybody alone."

"And we cannot spare a sled," Fargo pointed out.

"But I do not wish to go," Water-Song said.

"You don't understand," put in Fargo. "Today, we are turning off the Yukon and heading north, straight into the back country. It's killing land. We're looking for a gang of kidnappers and when we find them, those men are going to try to murder us. And I don't know why. And damn it, I need to know why. You can't come along. It is too risky."

"I must follow the red bear," Water-Song said simply. "That is my fate." She shrugged as if the matter were entirely decided and moved away from them toward the other sled.

"What she says is powerful medicine," White-Walker said, in the same resolute tone of voice. He also walked away from them and began hauling water for their sled dogs.

"Well," Sixty said. "I guess it's decided. That makes us four against twenty—"

The old man stopped abruptly when he spotted Count Victoroff heading their way, the fur collar of his coat turned up against the biting wind.

"So, Mr. Fargo," the count said, "today we leave the river and turn up the trail to find my dear Natasha." He rubbed his mittened hands together with glee. "We are so near! For six long months, I have dreamed of catching those runaway . . . those criminal kidnappers. And . . . rescuing my poor darling Natasha." Victoroff stopped, cleared his throat, and his piercing brown eyes regarded Fargo. "Now, where does this map say to go?"

"We'll head that way," Fargo said, "between those two cliffs." On the map, he pointed out two angular lines which seemed to indicate cliffs next to the broad line of the Yukon River. "We'll follow this up through the mountains," he said, his finger tracing the route, "until we get here. Looks like a big open valley. And there we'll make a camp. From that point, I'll scout alone, up further into the hills, until I've found them."

"Found them," the count repeated, in a quiet voice. Fargo noticed that Victoroff's fists were clenched and his dark eyes focused far away.

"You sure want that girl back," Fargo said.

"They must not get away with this," the count said in a low voice. "Anarchists! Criminals! They must be stopped!" He spun about on his heels and headed again toward his sled.

As he strapped on his snowshoes, Fargo took one last look across the wide Yukon River. It would be tough bushwhacking now. No broken trail, no river ice to speed them along. Just treacherous, snow-laden high country and hill after hill to climb. Two days of uphill travel until they reached the big valley. And then the real work would begin—the painstaking labor of tracking in high country, of walking mile after mile, day after day in wide, looping circles watching and listening for signs of human life, watching for the traces of the gang of Russian kidnappers hiding somewhere in the hills. And then what? What did Bull Slade and his men have up their sleeves and why? What was it all about?

All that day, Fargo with White-Walker beside him led the way up the winding narrow valleys between the snow-clad hills. All around them, the forest was black and dense with no sign of human life in the deepening winter stillness. It was slow-going on the snowshoes, breaking the trail between the tree trunks, finding the easiest way up the steepest slopes. Behind him, half of Slade's men followed, tamping down the trail so the dogs and sleds could pass. By nightfall, Fargo was exhausted and they had made a scant dozen miles. The next day, the trail turned upward and the tops of the distant peaks were bare and blue with snow. At midafternoon, they were moving across a small meadow when Fargo spotted tracks. He raised a hand and called a halt while he and White-Walker hastened forward to look. Behind them, Count Victoroff hurried forward from the line of sleds.

"Is it them?" he asked excitedly.

"Moose," Fargo said. "Fresh tracks." He and White-Walker looked toward the edge of the woods where the tracks led. Fargo raised his head and felt the wind blowing onto his face.

"Wind in good direction," White-Walker said. "And we will think like the moose."

"We're short of meat," Fargo said. "And there's only another hour of light.

"*Da, da,*" Victoroff said. "Let's hunt this moose."

Fargo, Sixty, White-Walker, and Count Victoroff fetched their rifles. Victoroff gave orders to Bull Slade and his men to pitch the camp to one side of the meadow and they were off.

The wind was blowing to the south and the moose had been heading west into the forest. Fargo led the way in a wide arc, circling downwind and backtracking toward the south. Count Victoroff halted for a moment, then followed, his rifle in hand and a puzzled look on his face.

"Where are we going?" he asked. "The moose has gone that direction."

"That moose has gone into the woods to look for something to eat," Sixty explained. "And once he's eaten, he'll double back along his own trail, downwind of it a bit. Then he'll rest. That way, he'll sniff out anything following his trail way before it can find him."

"I see," the count said thoughtfully. "But then, why are we heading this way?"

"We'll go out in a series of half-circles downwind of the trail," Sixty said. "We'll spot that resting moose before he gets a noseful of us. But, quiet. They've got good ears too."

Victoroff nodded silently as they entered the forest. Fargo came about in a second wide arc, and moved northward now by gentle degrees, quietly through the trees. The four of them, with the count lagging slightly behind, moved in a line through the still forest, eyes and ears alert. They had gone half a mile in a series of three arcs when Fargo raised his hand and they all came to a halt.

There, through the trees, was the dark shape of the magnificent beast, facing into the wind away from them. Fargo realized he'd have to get around the side of the moose in order to get a clear shot. He motioned for White-Walker to proceed to the moose's left with Sixty while he and the count took positions on the right. Slowly they moved apart, circling through the woods to surround the moose. The deep snow bent the branches of the spruce trees above them and the wind whistled in their faces.

Finally, they were close enough to the moose, standing still in the gathering dusk. Fargo paused with Victoroff underneath a huge spruce, its branches snow-laden. From here, Fargo saw, he could get a shot across the shoulder of the moose into its neck or head. He spotted White-Walker dim among the trees on the far side of the moose. Fargo raised his rifle as did the count. But Victoroff brought the barrel up too fast and high and it brushed against a branch of the spruce. With a soft swoosh, the snow cascaded off the branch and covered Victoroff, who swore softly in Russian. The moose's head shot up in alarm at the faint sound. At that instant, Fargo fired and heard two echoing shots from the direction of White-Walker and Sixty. The dark form of the moose took a faltering step forward, then staggered and fell.

Fargo hastened forward, leaving the count behind, dashing the snow out of his face. The moose lay on its side on the bloodstained snow, one dark eye staring blankly upward. It was a magnificent creature with a mammoth rack and huge shoulders and haunches, well muscled. Fargo felt a twinge of regret at having to kill it until he thought of the hungry dogs and their dwindling meat supply. By the time Victoroff came up to them, they had rolled the huge carcass onto a couple of large pine boughs and were preparing to drag it back through the forest. They took turns hauling the makeshift travois and approached camp just after dark.

As the camp came into sight, Fargo saw the men gathered around the fire in a huge crowd, chanting excitedly and shouting. Fargo smelled trouble and he hurried forward with Count Victoroff close on his heels.

"What is going on here?" Fargo shouted.

The men fell silent at the sound of his voice and shifted uncomfortably. The crowd broke up and at the center, Fargo saw Water-Song clutching her tunic, which had been ripped down the front. She spotted him and ran toward him. Fargo wrapped one arm around her and turned angrily toward the men.

Then he saw Bull Slade by the fire, his hands defiantly on his hips, a nasty sneer on his face.

"What the hell's happening here?"

"None of your business, Trailsman," Slade said.

"Are you all right?" Fargo asked Water-Song quietly. She was standing very close to him, clearly angry but not cowering.

"Yes," she said. "But I am glad you came now."

"Leave her alone, Slade," Fargo said, ice in his voice.

"Or what?" Slade shot back. "The boys and I were just having a little fun with your little girl. No harm intended."

Fargo moved toward Bull Slade. He'd had about all he could take of the bald man's taunts.

"Wait, wait!" Count Victoroff said, throwing himself between the two of them with his hands upheld. "Now, Mr. Slade. We will have no more of this. You hear me?"

Bull Slade's eyes narrowed as he regarded Victoroff for a long moment.

"Yeah, yeah," he said at last. "You're the boss." He turned away, sullen and angry. The men, muttering, moved off as well.

"I'm sorry, Mr. Fargo," Victoroff said. "Slade has not these good manners you have. But he is good to head an outfit. So I must keep him. I'm sure you understand."

"No," Fargo said. "I don't. He's lousy at leading

this outfit. He's hotheaded and careless. And he's a troublemaker to boot." Fargo looked around and saw that the men were out of earshot now. "And Slade wants us dead. You're crazy to keep that man around."

"Now, Mr. Fargo," Victoroff said, "I'm sure you have misunderstood Mr. Slade. It is just as I said. There is no reason in the world he would want to kill you or me or anyone. And, besides, I cannot exactly fire him in the middle of nowhere."

Fargo shrugged and turned away, pulling Water-Song with him. The count was just plain stupid and couldn't see danger if it hit him right in the face. As he moved toward their campfire, Fargo caught sight of Sixty pulling worriedly on his beard. But what held his attention was White-Walker. The tall Ingalik stood as if rooted to the spot, his black eyes fixed on Bull Slade with smoldering hatred.

Sitting around the fire that night, the three decided that Water-Song could not be left alone again in camp. Fargo gave her a knife for protection, which she slipped through a belt hidden beneath her tunic shirt. The only good news was that they no longer heard the wolves following. Apparently the pack had stayed down by the Yukon.

The following afternoon, Fargo called a halt at the crest of a hill and looked down into the wide snowy valley ringed by forested hills and high white peaks. Fargo scanned the land below, looking for signs of human habitation, the rising plume of smoke from a fire. But he saw nothing.

He pulled the buckskin map out again and studied it. At the far end of the valley lay a patch of rough snow where brambles and grass showed through. A marsh. The map had some wavy lines there and MacKenzie's trail led through the marsh and then the markings disappeared. Fargo looked up into the wooded hills above the marsh. They were somewhere up there, he knew. But where and how far? They had to move with care now in case the gang was close enough to spot their movements.

Close to the marsh, Fargo noticed a low hill with a rocky crest which protruded out into the valley. It was the perfect place for a base camp, on the south side, close in and sheltered from the wind. There, they would be out of sight if any of the kidnappers had a view of the valley. The hill would also provide a good lookout point and conceal the light from camp fire. And the back breeze, whistling over the rocky crest, would help disperse the telltale smoke.

Fargo led the way, keeping just inside the edge of the forest that hemmed the wide valley. In another hour they came around to the foot of the hill and struck out across the valley, sheltered from view. Camp was set up at the base of a tall cliff which would reflect some heat from the sun during the short days and from the campfire during the long, cold nights.

After a dinner of moose stew, Fargo wandered over to where Count Victoroff was sitting, taking an occasional swig from a fancy silver flask. Fargo sat and the count offered him the flask. The vodka burned like ice going down and then spread a warm glow along his limbs.

"Not bad," Fargo said, handing it back.

"Not bad? Only good vodka is Russian vodka," Victoroff said. "Only good book is Russian book. Only good woman is Russian woman." Victoroff raised the flask and took another swig.

"How about Russian kidnappers?" Fargo asked. The count's dark eyes glittered in the firelight. "There are some things you haven't told me yet. Like how many of them there are."

"Six," Victoroff said. "There are six of them."

"Only six? You sure of that?"

"Oh, yes. They are known to me. They were local . . . in the village. Peasants! Anarchists! Criminal elements!"

"So these six men, they were already in trouble with the law?"

Count Victoroff looked into the campfire and considered the question for a long minute.

"*Da*. Petty troubles," he said at last. "But always, I am wondering when they will be making trouble for me. Finally, they found this way. Kidnapping my Natasha. Right from my estate." Victoroff doffed his fur cap and raked his fingers through his thick wavy brown hair. His black brows were lowered.

"So, once I find their camp, Slade's men will move in," Fargo said. That was when the going would get rough. From what he overheard in the forest, Slade and his men would kill all of them as soon as they found the kidnappers. And although he'd tried to talk sense into Victoroff, the count still insisted on trusting Bull Slade. Now Victoroff called Slade over to join them.

Slade came reluctantly, pulling on his long black beard, his black eyes shining with hatred toward Fargo. He sat down and hunched toward the fire, warming his hands.

"We are just talking plans," Count Victoroff said. "You and your men will stay here in base camp while Fargo goes to find that gang."

"It might take a few days," Fargo warned them. "Even a week, if they're out there. This is rugged territory and I'll have to comb it pretty carefully if they're well hidden."

"You will find them as fast as possible," the count said. "I am sure. Then you will come back here and tell us where and Mr. Slade will take his men in to rescue Natasha."

"A surprise attack," Slade said. "We'll hit 'em hard with every rifle we've got."

"What about the girl?" Fargo asked, surprised. "You might catch her in the crossfire. You hit them with firepower and she's going to catch a stray bullet." The count looked unconcerned.

"You leave that to us, Fargo," Slade growled.

"*Da, da,*" Victoroff said. "Mr. Slade knows his business and you knows yours. Natasha will be fine. Everything will be fine."

"Sure," Fargo said. Victoroff seemed to have about as much sense as a potato. If he wanted his daughter in one piece, he was sending in the wrong men to do the job. But there was nothing he could say that was going to change either of their minds. And for the life of him, Fargo couldn't guess why

Slade might want the rest of them dead—and Natasha too by the sound of things.

Fargo returned to the other campfire and sat brooding by the warm flames. White-Walker and Water-Song had constructed a couple of sturdy wickiups of tree boughs reinforced by lengths of canvas. Now they were throwing ropes over the branches of trees and suspending the supplies and joints of moose meat high off the ground out of the reach of wandering predators. Sixty looked up from oiling his rifle.

"You're a bundle of chuckles tonight," he said.

"This whole thing stinks to hell," Fargo said. He threw a twig into the fire, where it crackled and spat. Sixty nodded agreement. "I just wish I could figure it out." Just then, they heard Water-Song giggle and they looked up to see her hauling a moose haunch higher and higher. Sixty followed the direction of Fargo's gaze toward her slim figure. "Look," Fargo said, "I need you to stay in camp with Water-Song."

"Yeah," Sixty said with a sigh. "I kinda figured that was coming. I guess White-Walker's faster than me at this point. But, damn it, I'd like to get my hands on whoever strung up Petie-Boy."

"We all would," Fargo said. "The other thing I want you to do is to keep your ears open. Slade said he was planning to do us all in as soon as I found the girl. Victoroff seems to think I heard wrong. But we've got to be ready."

Sixty thought for a minute and then brightened.

"I'll stick a cache out in the woods," he said. "Water-Song and I'll do it little by little starting tomorrow. The extra snowshoes, meat, matches, knives, rifles, blankets, clothing. That way, if things get rough we can rendezvous there and get the hell out of here. Just in case."

"Just in case," Fargo said, patting him on the back. "Good plan."

It was getting late and there would be a long day ahead of them. Fargo and Water-Song entered one of the wickiups which stood close to the cliff. Inside he found she had spread branches under the thick layers of bearskins. The canvas kept the wind out and in a few moments the interior was warmed by their heat. Fargo pulled off his moccasins and parka and snuggled down under the robes, holding her close. They made love again, slowly, and he tasted the sweetness of her familiarity. Afterward, she wrapped her arms around his neck.

"I am afraid for you, Fargo," she murmured.

"I'm afraid for all of us," he replied. "Sixty is staying in camp with you tomorrow. But I want you to be careful. Stay close to him or inside the wickiup. Slade and his men are animals and you're not safe here."

"I know," she said. "I will use the knife if I have to."

Fargo fell into an uneasy sleep and dreamed of tracking a red bear through the forest but each time he drew near and raised his rifle, it turned into Victoroff.

Fargo and White-Walker moved silently up the hillside. It had been three days since they had left base camp and they had scoured the hills above the marsh, moving through the trees as silently as deer, sometimes stopping and standing for long minutes to listen and watch. But they had heard and seen nothing of the gang of kidnappers. Now they were heading up into the higher country.

They gained the top of the crest and entered a narrow, high valley. Fargo spotted a herd of antelope grazing where some of the summer grasses poked through the wind-swept snow. His trigger finger itched but he did not shoot. The retort of a rifle would be heard for miles around and right now they were after bigger game.

All day, they moved slowly through the valley, keeping under cover of the trees, trying to walk where the snow was blown to leave as little track as possible. They found nothing but an abundance of game. Threaded throughout the wooded hillsides were rabbit runs. A herd of deer moved through the trunks of the trees. The valley was rich with meat and would make a perfect hideout.

But by late afternoon they still had seen nothing. Fargo stood for a moment looking around. Where to now? The valley seemed to be a dead end.

"I have a feeling about this place," Fargo said.

"I too," White-Walker agreed.

They decided to camp for the night at one side of the valley and keep watch one more day. They were tracking Indian style—no fire, no tents. The only food was pemmican and berries packed in seal oil. As darkness fell, they found a deep snowbank beneath some snow-laden trees and fell to digging sleeping holes, as the sled dogs did. Without a campfire, the evening wind was unbearably bitter and every night they had retired early as soon as the light faded, creeping into the snowbanks like hibernating bears. Tonight, as Fargo lay curled up snugly in the ice cavern warmed by his breath, he wondered how close they were to the gang's hideout. It could be dozens of miles away or just over the next rise.

The dawn was still blue when they rose. A light snow was falling. More was coming in. Fargo measured the thick gray clouds overhead, wondering how heavy the snowfall would get. On one hand, fresh snow would hide any tracks they might have left through the woods. But it would also fill in the tracks they were seeking. They strapped on their snowshoes, then shook the overhanging branches of the trees until the piles of snow cascaded down onto the snow-bank, obliterating all traces of their sleeping holes.

Fargo took another long look around the narrow valley, measuring again the high chasm at the head of the valley, which seemed to be a dead end. He led the way uphill. The snow fell with a quiet hiss around them. White-Walker dragged a pine branch behind them to partially obscure the tracks of their snowshoes.

They had nearly reached the top of the valley when Fargo saw it. Something out of place up ahead. He held up his hand and White-Walker came to a halt behind him. They both listened carefully. Then Fargo moved forward only a few feet until he had a good look at what he had spotted.

A rabbit in its white winter coat hung by one foot against a small sapling. Someone had set a snare along the rabbit run, a bent sapling barely held by a thong of babiche which a scurrying rabbit would trip. The babiche loop would tighten around the rabbit as the bent sapling sprang upward. The dead rabbit would be suspended above the ground, out of reach of every wandering animal except the grizzly.

And whoever had set the rabbit snare would be back to check on it. Fargo did not move closer, but turned and scanned about him. White-Walker pointed silently to a thicket nearby and Fargo nodded. They retreated, dragging branches across their tracks and gathering other branches for camouflage. When they reached the thicket, Fargo spread their blankets on the ground while White-Walker expertly propped the branches about them, forming a natural-looking blind. Someone would practically have to stumble on top of them to find their hiding place.

They waited through the long afternoon, occasionally stretching their tired aching muscles but thankful for the falling snow and the lack of biting wind. They dared not move from the blind since they would disturb the fresh snow that had fallen around them and would make their hiding place conspicuous. Finally, in the late afternoon, just as Fargo was beginning to think they might have to retreat down the hill for the night, he heard a faint sound.

White-Walker glanced at him and they slowly parted the branches and looked out toward the rabbit snare. In another moment, Fargo spotted a short stocky figure approaching, coming downhill. The man moved quickly and well on his snowshoes but Fargo could see nothing of his face since he was well bundled up. The man paused at the snare, cut the rabbit down with a swift flick of his knife, reset the snare and moved off through the trees. They heard him cutting down another rabbit not far away and they sat still, hardly breathing until the sounds died away. Only then did they rise and strap on their snowshoes again and followed the trail. The fresh tracks were easy to follow, even in the dusk, but Fargo realized that by morning the falling snow would have filled them in again.

They moved slowly through the gathering darkness, careful not to get within earshot of the man. They passed a dozen or more rabbit snares, all reset and ranged along the top of the valley. At last, the track led abruptly upward, seeming to head straight into a sheer cliff. As they drew closer, the sheer rock wall loomed up above them, over the tops of the trees, but suddenly, Fargo saw a slice of sky between the towering rocks and realized there was a narrow passageway. It had to be the entrance to the kidnappers' hideout.

Fargo glanced at White-Walker and the Ingalik nodded. There was hardly a need for words. White-Walker always seemed to anticipate his every move. They waited at the edge of the dark trees for more than an hour as the darkness fell completely. And then they moved in.

The opening between the rocks was wide enough for four men to walk abreast. But plenty narrow for an ambush, Fargo thought. He drew his knife. His rifle, slung over his shoulder, would be useless in the closeness of the gap. Would they keep a guard at the entrance? Fargo moved forward, eyes and ears alert to any sound. Behind him, White-Walker followed silently. They had gone a short way when suddenly the walls fell away and Fargo saw a second valley, smaller than the one below, open up before them. On one side he spotted a large log cabin with a smaller barn off to the rear. Rising into the night sky were sparks from the chimney and two square windows glowed faintly.

"Jackpot," Fargo whispered to himself. They stood hidden in a rock crevice for a while looking at the cabin as darkness came on and Fargo realized they needed to find a place to rest. But he also wanted to keep watch over the cabin. Hesitant to dig any snow holes so close to the cabin, Fargo pointed back toward the tall rocks which were riddled with pockets where they might find shelter. In minutes, White-Walker had located a round, dry cave, fifteen feet up the rock, out of the wind with a lip that would afford them some cover from view. Fargo clambered up to join him and they portioned out the pemmican and berries, then sat for a time, wrapped in blankets and looking out toward the cabin.

"Tomorrow we will see how many men," White-Walker said softly. "And if woman is there."

"Right," Fargo said. His mind was racing ahead and he was imagining leading Bull Slade and his men back to this place. Slade had said he was going to pour every bullet they had into their hide-out. It was a damn stupid plan, ham-handed, and Fargo knew it meant the girl Natasha would die one way or the other. And if Count Victoroff had been so concerned about his daughter, why hadn't that worried him? Fargo fell asleep puzzling over it all again.

At the crack of dawn, Fargo lay watching the cabin. Just as the sky was lightening, the door opened and two men came out. One of them looked like the stocky figure they'd seen collecting the rabbits the day before. The two men made some trips inside, hauling firewood, and then the stocky one set to chopping some logs with an ax. The other one cleaned rabbits and then stored the meat in a cache that stood out by the barn, elevated on high stilts off the ground. Meanwhile, the chimney smoked and Fargo raised his face to the wind. Bacon? He was sure he could smell that in the smoke. After more than an hour of work, the door opened again.

Fargo and White-Walker exchanged swift glances as they spotted a small woman with long shining blond hair. She held up a tin pot and beat on it twice with a spoon, then laughed as the stocky man threw down his ax and ran toward the house. When he reached her he tried to grab the pot from her hand but she laughed again and held them out of reach until the other man came and grabbed them from her. She laughingly pulled them both into the cabin and the door closed.

Fargo rested back against the rock and thought over what he'd just seen. Natasha—if that was Natasha—didn't look too unhappy. In fact the three of them acted more like a family than like kidnappers and hostage. But then, maybe she was just making the best of it, hoping to eventually get away. And they had only seen two men. Where were the other four? All that day, Fargo and White-Walker waited in the rock hollow, watching the two men and Natasha go about their daily activities. One of the men was hauling or chopping wood continuously all day, adding to the huge neat woodpile behind the cabin. They also busied themselves with a pair of goats which they brought out of the barn, milked, and let gambol about. They set a wooden rack out in the sun and strung what looked like strips of salmon and meat over it to air dry. At midday, when the sun was strongest, the woman sat outside by the cabin for a while and sewed on a quilt.

In the late afternoon, a light snow began falling again. The three went inside again and then the two men emerged with rifles and bow and arrows, dressed for hunting. Fargo and White-Walker huddled down in the rock cavern as they heard the sounds of the two men walking just below them on their way out of the valley. Fargo realized how clever they had been. They were going to hunt with arrows which would make no sound and which, if found, would be assumed to be Ingalik, and they carried their rifles only for emergencies. And he realized that they had kept the fire out all day so that the rising plume of smoke would not betray their presence for miles around. And they were going out to hunt as the snow was falling so that once again their tracks would be hidden within hours of their return.

White-Walker and Fargo waited for several minutes after the men had passed by. And then, by silent looks, they agreed that White-Walker would remain behind at the entrance in case the men came back while Fargo would go talk to Natasha. At least he could try to get the girl away from the cabin before Slade came in with all his guns.

In the gathering dusk, Fargo made his way across the small valley, heading toward the cabin. When he reached it, he drew close to one of the windows and looked inside. It was a large room, cheery and crowded with shelves of supplies and chairs and several beds covered with furs and blankets. Natasha sat by the table on which were several candles. Her golden head was bent over her sewing. Fargo moved toward the door and put his hand on the latch, pressing very gently. It lifted with scarcely a sound and he pushed open the door.

The flames on the candles suddenly danced in the cold air and Natasha spoke a sentence in Russian. When Fargo didn't answer, she looked up at him, then leaped to her feet to see him standing there.

"Natasha?" he said with a smile. He didn't want to scare her. "I am a friend." Her eyes narrowed and she backed away, her sewing clutched in front of her, fear on her face.

"I am a friend," Fargo tried again. He stepped further into the cabin. "Please don't be afraid. You understand English?"

Natasha hesitated a moment and her eyes flickered toward the door.

"Yes. I understand," she said. "Who are you?"

"My name is Skye Fargo."

At the mention of his name, she looked surprised.

"Skye Fargo?" she repeated. "You are friend to Pete MacKenzie? He told me about you. He is come here too?"

Fargo hesitated, not wanting to tell her about MacKenzie's death but she read the unease in his expression and her face grew troubled.

"But MacKenzie, he sent you here. No?"

"In a manner of speaking," he said.

Natasha looked puzzled. She tossed her long hair and smiled at him.

"What this mean? In a manner of speaking? You say yes or no?"

"Sorry," Fargo said. "I meant to say yes, I came because of Pete. But he didn't send me. I'm here to rescue you. Your father—he is here and he sent me."

"My father is dead," Natasha said. "I don't know what you are talking about."

"Count Victoroff sent me to find you."

Natasha's eyes grew wide with horror as if she had seen a ghost. And with lightning speed, she darted toward the door, flinging it open and grabbing a rifle from beside the door. Fargo barely had time to grab one of her wrists as she stumbled outside.

"Hold on, there," he said. "Wait a minute."

The rifle barrel was wavering skyward and he made a grab for it, but she pulled the trigger. The gunfire exploded through the silence and echoed off the towering rocks. She struggled for the gun again, but Fargo wrenched it from her grasp and threw it aside, grabbing her around the waist and holding her close to him.

"Now, I need some answers," he said in her ear. "And I need them now. Before there's a blood-bath."

But he realized it was too late. From beyond the rocks, Fargo heard the sound of an answering rifle. And he knew the two men were heading back their way.

6

Fargo listened as the sounds of the distant rifle died away. The sound could be heard for a great distance as it echoed up the valley and through the still air.

"Now, tell me," Fargo said impatiently. "If Count Victoroff isn't your father, then who is he?"

"No, no," Natasha sobbed, writhing and trying to free herself from his grasp. "My father is dead. And I will never go back. Never. And I will not let Dmitry and Ivan go. They will not go. Never."

"So, who is Victoroff?" he persisted.

Natasha raised her tearstained face to him.

"Don't you understand?" she said. "There is nothing we can do. He is boyar. He is important aristocrat. And we are serfs. Belong to his estate in the Ukraine. Count Victoroff killed my father."

Fargo nodded and let go of her. It all made sense now. The whole goddamned mess. They were escaped serfs and Victoroff wanted them back. Or even wanted them dead.

"And he was . . . it was . . ." Natasha bit her lip, unwilling to go on.

"What?" he prodded gently. "Something about Victoroff?" She nodded, embarrassed.

"Droit de seigneur," she said at last, not meeting his eyes. "This is old custom. Mostly died out but Victoroff he wants this right again. I refuse and he is angry. So angry he killed my poor papa."

Fargo had heard of it before. The nobility's privilege to deflower any of the peasant women on their estates. It was a brutal rule that nobody followed anymore. But Victoroff had thought he could get away with it apparently.

"But my brothers," Natasha said. "Dmitry and Ivan . . ."

"Those two men you're with?" Fargo asked.

"Yes," she said. "They said no. Victoroff cannot do this. They said they would take me away to the America wilderness where we will all be safe. Some others escape with us. Four more from our village."

"What happened to them?" Fargo asked.

"They ran away," Natasha said. "The day that MacKenzie found us. They were afraid Victoroff would find us. But my brothers and I, we explain everything to this Pete MacKenzie. He tells us he thought I was Victoroff's daughter. He is a good man. He says he will go back and tell the big boss that I am not daughter. He says he and the boss will try to stop Victoroff." She spat the words angrily. "Daughter! I, Victoroff daughter? He is pig!"

"Yeah," Fargo said. "He told me the same story. And I guess when MacKenzie told the big boss, he got killed for it."

"MacKenzie? Dead?" Natasha shook her head sadly. "He was good man. Like you."

Just then gunfire erupted at the entrance to the valley. Fargo let go of Natasha and ran toward the sound. He could hear her behind him calling out in Russian, no doubt telling her brothers not to shoot.

When he arrived at the gap, Fargo was astonished to see White-Walker standing with his foot on one of the Russians, rifle pointed at his head, while the other stood by helplessly, weaponless and afraid to move for fear of his brother's safety. The snow was falling steadily now as the dusk drew in around them.

"Let him up," Fargo said.

White-Walker's brows raised but he complied and the stocky man got to his feet angrily, then made a lunge for his rifle, which lay nearby. Natasha came running up, babbling in Russian. The stocky man paused, then glanced at Fargo as his sister's words sank in.

"You friend of MacKenzie?" he said slowly. Fargo nodded. "I am Dmitry Rachlevsky." The stocky man pumped Fargo's hand enthusiastically. "This my brother, Ivan."

"This is White-Walker," Fargo said. "Also friend of MacKenzie's." Fargo noticed that Natasha was shivering in the cold, having come out without her parka. He pulled a pack down from their sleeping place and threw a blanket to her, which she wrapped around herself gratefully.

"You are welcome here," Dmitry said, waving his arm around the small valley. "Here we hide from bad count."

"How long you plan on staying here?" Fargo asked.

"Maybe just one year more," Dmitry said. "Maybe two. I have friends, important friends in

Moscow. They say Tsar make big reforms. Give land to the workers. Free the serfs like in other countries. But, maybe it doesn't come soon. We wait. When serfs are free, Victoroff can do nothing to us. Until then, we stay here in secret."

"My brother and I are very careful," Ivan said. "No traces do we leave in the snow. No one can find us."

"We found you," Fargo said. "And the sound of that gunfire might have carried down the valley. Victoroff is down there with about twenty men."

At this news, Natasha jumped and the two Rachlevsky brothers exchanged worried glances.

"Victoroff? Here? In valley? So close?" Dmitry said with a quaver in his voice. The three were plainly terrified of the count. A swirl of snow blew around them. Fargo gazed across the valley toward the little cabin, which was disappearing in the whiteness.

"They probably won't move in this storm," Fargo said. "And from the looks of it, it's going to keep up for a while."

"Come inside," Dmitry said, gesturing toward the cabin. Fargo and White-Walker gathered up their packs and followed the three Rachlevskys and entered the warm, close cabin. Natasha exclaimed sharply and ran to the stove, where a large iron pot was exuding a delicious-smelling steam.

"Oh! My borscht! Is ruined?" She lifted the top off the pot and then smiled as she stirred it with a long-handled spoon.

"Please, make comfortable," Dmitry said, waving Fargo and White-Walker toward a thick wooden table surrounded by chairs. For the next several hours, Fargo forgot everything as they drank good Russian vodka, ate borscht, boiled potatoes, deer stew, and thick chewy black bread. The two Rachlevsky brothers told stories of hunting Russian black bears in the Ukraine forests and White-Walker told of summer moose hunts along the Yukon. Natasha, sitting next to Fargo, glanced at him often. She was very beautiful, her brown eyes like liquid pools and her long blond silken hair reaching to her slender waist. She had changed to a low-cut blouse that showed the curves of her full, high breasts.

"You are very quiet man," she said softly to him while Ivan was telling a tale.

"Guess I'm just taking in the scenery," he said with a smile. He reached toward her and caught up a lock of her hair, holding it toward the candlelight where it gleamed golden. He let it go again and she blushed.

"Where do you live?" she asked. "Down in Alakanuk?"

"Nowhere," he said.

"Everyone live somewhere," she said, clucking her tongue.

"Folks call me the Trailsman," he explained. "I'm always on the move."

"*Da,*" Natasha said thoughtfully. "We have such wandering men in Ukraine too."

When the meal was finished, Ivan proudly carried out a small samovar, poured in water and tea and lit the flame beneath it. Soon the contraption was hissing merrily and Dmitry poured them all a cup of tea, sweetened with a teaspoonful of jam.

Afterward, they rose. There wasn't enough room in the small cabin for all of them, so Fargo and White-Walker decided to sleep in the shelter of the barn. Fargo felt Natasha's eyes following him as he and Ingalik left the cabin and plunged into the swirling snow.

The blizzard was a heavy one. For a moment, Fargo wondered if keeping watch at the entrance to the hideaway would even be necessary. Surely Victoroff and his men couldn't track them in this snow. Still, all night as they sat in the cabin eating and drinking, he'd felt uneasy, as if Victoroff were even now coming after them through the howling gusts. It was impossible, but Fargo had to trust his instincts. He volunteered to take the first watch and White-Walker went into the barn, carrying a small tin oil stove Dmitry gave them which would provide light and a little heat.

Fargo hoisted his pack on his back and trudged away through the deep drifted snow and darkness toward the gap. He climbed up to the rock hollow and crawled inside, hunched against the cold stone wall, and wrapped himself in a couple of blankets. From here he could keep an eye on the passageway below. As the cold hours passed, he thought of Victoroff, how the count's lies had trapped him into hunting down the Rachlevskys. And now there was no doubt in his mind that Bull Slade had been responsible for the murder of Pete MacKenzie. And he also understood why the Russian shopkeeper at Alakanuk and the Russian traders at the post had been so angry at Victoroff. They had all known the count was chasing run-away serfs.

But what to do now? If he and White-Walker returned to camp and told where they'd found the Rachlevskys, they'd be killed just as Pete MacKenzie had been. Victoroff and Slade had probably banked on the fact that there were six men with Natasha and they had figured Fargo and White-Walker, being outnumbered, wouldn't get close enough to any of them to find out the real story.

For long hours, Fargo's thoughts ran back and forth as he tried to make out how to save the Rachlevskys from Count Victoroff. How to get Sixty and Water-Song spirited away from Victoroff's base camp. How to get revenge on the count and on Buck Slade. It would be damn hard against twenty trail-hardened men. But toward morning, a plan began to take shape in his mind.

Now it was time for sleep. Fargo climbed down out of the rock and made his way to the barn. The snow was thick and drifted, still coming down fast. Inside the barn, it was warm and smelled of goats. White-Walker awoke, dressed, and left to take over the watch. As Fargo stripped off his snowy parka and moccasins, he looked about. By the golden light of the small tin stove, he could see the inside of the large barn, the stalls for the goats and the large piles of silage for them to eat all winter. The barn was constructed of logs, with the chinks firmly packed with mud. The Rachlevskys were hard workers, he thought. They didn't deserve to go back into servitude. He threw himself down on a pile of dried grass and sleep came on fast.

Fargo awoke when he heard a soft bump against the door. The wind was moaning outside. He sat up and stretched as the door opened and a shaft of silvery morning light entered the barn along with a swirl of snow. A small bundled figure carrying a pail came inside and Fargo saw that it was Natasha. She paused at the door and struggled out of her parka, then shook her long blond hair about her.

"Good morning!" she said brightly. "Snow very deep. Like in Ural Mountains back home. Where is your Indian friend?"

"He's keeping watch at the entrance," Fargo said. "I did the first half of the night."

"Keeping watch? You think anybody could come in such snow?"

"I don't know," Fargo said. All night, his dreams had been full of Count Victoroff and of Water-Song calling for help. Dark, disturbing dreams.

Natasha crossed the room and turned up the oil stove. She set the pail down beside him.

"Hot water to wash," she said. "After you use, I will give rest to goats."

Fargo stripped off his shirt and dashed the water over his face and neck. He paused to notice her standing watching him, her eyes on his muscular chest and powerful arms. She blushed and moved toward the stalls, taking down an empty bucket from a nail. As Fargo finished his washing up, Natasha milked the goats one by one, let them out of their stalls to walk around and eat the silage. She lined up the two buckets of steaming fresh goat's milk by the door as Fargo was buttoning up his shirt.

"Poor goats," she said, as one of them playfully butted her. "All long winter they must stay in this barn because it is too cold outside." She glanced at him, her eyes soft, and he read the longing in them that she could not speak, the longing that he had seen the night before.

Fargo crossed to her and pulled her gently toward him. She came, unresisting, eager, as he folded her into his arms. He held her face between his hands and gazed into her deep brown eyes. Her eyes said yes and he bent over her, kissing her lightly at first, then more deeply as her mouth opened to him and he slid his tongue between her lips. She seemed surprised for a moment, then moaned softly and he ran his fingers through the coolness of her silken hair, massaging her neck, her shoulders, stroking down the curve of her waist and hips.

She pulled away for a moment and looked up at him, her eyes sad and serious.

"We are going to die, aren't we?" Natasha said. "Count Victoroff is going to find us and kill us. Isn't that right?"

"No," Fargo said. "We'll find a way around the count. Don't worry about dying. Not anytime soon."

"I am afraid," she said, clinging to him. "And . . . I have never known . . . about love." She buried her face in his broad chest and did not meet his eyes. "I do not want to die and not know this thing."

Fargo tightened his arms around her and lifted her chin so he could look again into her eyes.

"I'm not the kind of man who settles down," he said gently. "You know that."

"Da," she said. "But, please, Skye. Show me this thing. Show me how."

Fargo crossed to the door and shot home the bolt. He led her to the large pile of dried grass and they lay down. Once again, he kissed her, her mouth, her eyelids, her neck. She clung to him, panting softly and he slowly unfastened the buttons on her tunic. She did not look up at him as he opened her blouse and he saw her full high breasts, pale white and pink-tipped. He brushed against one of her nipples and she shivered as it came erect. He took the nipple between his lips and flicked his tongue over it.

"Oh, oh, ah," Natasha moaned, writhing from side to side. He gently kneaded her other breast in his hand and she shivered. He could feel his hardness straining against his jeans, hot and throbbing to be inside her, but he knew he had to be slow with her.

He unbuttoned her skirt and she helped him ease it down over her slender flanks along with her pantaloons and then she lay white and tender and naked before him, the pale golden triangle between her legs gleaming in the golden light from the small stove.

Fargo gently laid his hand on her knee and moved it upward, slowly, slowly as she caught her breath and opened her legs to him until his fingers brushed against her fur, then her wetness. He rubbed the folded lips, finding her swollen button and massaging it slowly.

"Ah! Ah!" Natasha said, moving under him. With his other hand he unfastened his jeans and stripped them off, his erectness huge and ready.

He pulled her hand toward him and she hesitatingly touched him, gasped, then held him in her hand, her eyes wide.

"You want?" he whispered in her ear.

"*Da*, yes, yes, I am ready," she said, her breath in ragged gasps.

Fargo moved his hand to her again and gently inserted his fingers inside her wetness, moving so slowly until she gave way. Natasha stifled a cry and he moved his fingers away, rubbing her again. She relaxed, moved under him, her hard knob engorged and ready. She tightened her hand on him, stroking him hesitantly, shyly. Fargo lifted himself above her and paused at her entrance, then pushed inside her, slowly, inch by inch, feeling her tight and wet and warm around him.

"Oh, oh . . ." she breathed, her brown eyes wide, her legs open to him as he slipped into her sheath. He began to pump into her, slowly at first, then faster, pulling her hips toward him as he felt the urgency gathering in him. Natasha pushed upward to meet his every thrust, hesitant at first, then more confidently. He moved his hand between them and found her button, rubbed against it again, and she shuddered. He was pumping hard into her now, his huge shaft hot and ready as he felt her trembling all over as though shaken by an earthquake.

"AHHHHHH!" she suddenly screamed, her legs coming up around him as she shook uncontrollably, and he felt the contractions within her like sucking ocean waves pulling on him, tightening in rings around him as she came. Fargo let go, shot his hotness hard and fast into her, felt the release of everything as he pumped again, and again, driving deep up into her, pulling her hips down toward him, one hand on her soft breast. Again and again until he was dry, and then he stopped and fell onto the soft dry grass beside her.

Natasha curled up beside him and he put his hand between her breasts. Her heart beat as fast as a small bird's.

"Thank you," she said, her brown eyes grave again. "Now if I die, I will know this loving."

Fargo kissed her face gently, pulled the long golden waves of hair from off her bare shoulder and kissed her there too.

"You are not going to die," he said. "I'll see to that."

After a few more minutes, they rose. They washed from the pail of water, which was now cool, and dressed. Fargo was just pulling on his parka when he heard a sound over the groan of the blizzard. A distant sound. Fargo swore and threw open the door. He could hardly see the cabin because the snow was coming down so hard. He listened and heard it again. But the falling snow was muffling the sound and the wind was whistling and the pine trees were creaking. Something was wrong. He knew that much.

"Come on," he called to Natasha. She bent to pick up the buckets of goat's milk, but he pulled her away and out of the door. As they dashed for the cabin, Fargo kept listening. But he didn't hear anything again. Something was out there. And it could only be Victoroff.

Only Dmitry was inside the cabin, sitting at the table drinking tea. He looked up surprised when they stumbled inside.

"Where's Ivan?" Fargo asked.

"Gone to get rabbits," Dmitry said.

"I think there's trouble," Fargo snapped. "I hope I'm wrong about this, but I heard something from the direction of the gap. White-Walker's out there. And so's Ivan. Get some supplies and snowshoes, a couple of packs. We may have to move out now."

Natasha looked scared but did as he ordered. Dmitry started to protest, then fell to helping her. In minutes, they had loaded three packs with some pemmican, blankets, and other supplies and had dressed in their warmest gear. Just as they finished, Fargo eased open the door and listened again. Then he heard it again. This time, closer. Unmistakable. Two men's voices calling to one another. White-Walker wasn't one for shouting. So he was right. They'd been found. Fargo swore and shut the door.

"Is there a back way out of here?" he asked.

"Little window," Dmitry said.

"Let's go," Fargo snapped. "They're close enough now that they'll catch us if we go out the front. Fargo bolted the door and Dmitry threw back the inside wooden shutters on the back window and then pushed it open and unfastened the shutters on the outside. They had to take off their packs to fit through, but in a minute

Dmitry and his sister stood beside the small cabin.

"Don't bother putting on your snowshoes yet," Fargo said in a low voice as he handed the rifles through to them. "Just head up into those trees and wait. I'll catch up with you."

He could hear the muffled voices of the count's men now, several coming from the near distance. He couldn't make out the words but they sounded excited. They had probably spotted the cabin and were in the process of rounding up everybody else for an attack. Fargo hoisted himself out the window and pulled the interior shutters closed, shut the window, then bolted shut the outer shutters as well. He dashed some snow across the outside shutters until he could hardly tell they had been disturbed. Then he pulled a blanket out of his pack and swept it across the snow they had trampled down while getting out of the window. If Victoroff and his men didn't spot their tracks, they had a chance to get away.

Fargo retreated up the hillside behind the cabin, dragging the blanket behind him to disguise his tracks. With the snow falling so fast and the wind blasting, it would be a matter of minutes before the tracks were obliterated completely. He had just reached the first of the tall spruces at the edge of the woods when he spotted something moving below him. He ducked behind the tree and peered out. Below he saw the murky shape of three men emerge from one side of the cabin and take positions around the back. He'd been right. They had the cabin surrounded.

Then he heard his name being called. It was muffled through the fast-falling snow but he heard it.

"Hey, Fargo!" the voice shouted. "We know you're in there."

The voice was unmistakably Bull Slade's.

"Come on out or we'll shoot your Indian pal here."

Fargo gritted his teeth in fury. Staying in the cover of the trees, he made his way through the edge of the forest until he could see the snow-dimmed group of figures standing out in the open in front of the cabin. Two men had hold of White-Walker, one to each arm. Bull Slade stood behind the three of them. He raised his rifle.

"Come on, Fargo. Show yourself or we shoot this redskin."

Fargo pulled up his Sharps and took aim, but Slade took a step to one side and Fargo lost his clear shot. There was no way. He shifted his aim to one of the men holding White-Walker. The instant he squeezed the trigger, White-Walker, as if he sensed what Fargo was doing, sprang to one side, barreling into the second man as Fargo's bullet felled the first. There was a sudden crack of rifle fire and White-Walker staggered, took a hesitating step toward Bull Slade, and then dropped onto the snow. He was dead. Fargo knew it for sure. He swore and shifted his aim dead center to Bull Slade, then fired but the shot went too high. Bull Slade yowled and clutched his shoulder. He'd been winged. He and the other man made a run for cover while Fargo reloaded.

By the time he could fire again, Slade was behind some trees.

"Get him! Get that bastard!" Slade screamed at the top of his lungs. "I'll get you, Fargo, if I have to wrench your neck with my bare hands!"

"He's up in the woods!" The voice was booming over the cover of some rocks near the cabin, but Fargo knew whose it was. It was Count Victoroff. And now they knew right where he was.

Fargo strapped on his snowshoes now as a few bullets whizzed through the trees nearby. They didn't have him pinned down exactly, but as soon as the men came swarming up the hillside, they'd be trapped. He strode up the hill through the snow, moving fast, looking around for Natasha and her brother. He hadn't gone far when he heard a whistle.

"Over here!" Dmitry called out.

Fargo headed toward the voice and found them huddled between three tall spruce trees.

"Is there any way out of this valley besides that gap?" Fargo asked.

"*Nyet,*" Dmitry said. "Is very safe valley."

"Then we'll have to shoot our way out," Fargo said. "They'll be heading up the hill after us." He thought for a moment then had an idea.

Below, he heard the voices of the men as they came up through the trees, spread out, searching the hillside for them. There was no time to lose.

"Follow me," he said. They moved across the hill toward the gap and Fargo saw a large outcropping with a narrow crevice. "Stay here until the men pass by," he said, pushing them into it. "Then head right for the gap. It will be guarded, but when I get there, we'll shoot our way out."

Then Fargo descended a dozen yards and secreted himself behind a tree as he heard the line of men coming on, closer and closer. They were bound to search the rock outcropping because it was a natural hiding place. But with luck, his plan would work.

In a minute, through the descending curtain of snow, he caught sight of three men coming up the hill, spread out in a line. He couldn't make out any of their faces because of the blinding whiteness. He waited until they had drawn even with him and he stepped out from the cover of the tree, falling in line with them.

"Up there!" Fargo called out after a moment, keeping his voice gruff.

"Where?" one of the men shouted.

"I see them over that way!" Fargo answered. He pointed off to the east away from the outcropping. "There they go!" He broke into an awkward run and his shouts were taken up by the men in the line. In a moment, they were all following him, strung out behind as they staggered up the hillside, fighting the heavy drifted snow.

"I don't see them!" one shouted.

"Right up there!" Fargo said. "Just disappeared over that ridge!"

"Yeah!" another shouted back. "I saw 'em! I saw 'em!"

Fargo dropped back as the men surged around him, pushing themselves up the hillside through the snow. In another moment, their gray figures had disappeared and Fargo turned about, hurrying downhill. He passed the rock outcropping and saw the dim tracks, already drifted by the wind, heading toward the gap. He followed.

He had almost reached the rocky gap when he spotted Dmitry and Natasha hunched down behind a snow-covered log. He joined them.

"Three men," Dmitry said.

"Good," said Fargo. He looked over the situation. One man was poised on the top of the rocky gap keeping watch. Two others walked back and forth warily below, their rifles at the ready. "When I start to shoot, you take out the one up there," Fargo said. Dmitry nodded.

Fargo got to his feet and ducked for cover, then came out of the forest at a run.

"Hey! Victoroff says he needs reinforcements!" he shouted to the two men on the ground. "They've got the girl cornered up on the hill."

"All right," one of the two men said and started to move away. Just then, he turned back and Fargo could see the suspicion.

"Hey . . ." the man said, raising his rifle. But Fargo was too fast. He pulled up his Sharps and blasted. The man clutched his belly and pitched backward into the snow. Just then the crack of a second shot came from Dmitry's direction and the man standing high on the rock overhead fell headlong downward onto the snow and landed with a bone-crunching snap. He jerked once and then lay still. The second man, who was holding his rifle by the barrel, was caught by surprise. He swung it out suddenly in Fargo's direction, but Fargo caught the butt and wrested it from the man's grasp and wrenched it free.

Fargo kicked out and caught the man in the belly. He went down and came up with a long knife in hand, hell in his eyes, and slashing the air. Fargo kicked out again, catching the man's knife, which went flying. Then he followed with a shattering swing of the rifle butt through the air which caught the man full in the face and his head snapped backward and he crumpled and did not move again.

"Let's get out of here," Fargo said as Dmitry and Natasha came running up. There was no time to lose. In moments, the count and his men, having heard the gunfire at the gap, would realize the ruse and would be pouring down the hillside after them. The three of them couldn't possibly hold out against all those men in a shoot-out. They'd have to make a run for it. In the deep snow, they couldn't move fast but then neither could their pursuers.

The three of them moved out the gap and Fargo led as they headed down the hillside. Dmitry was good on snowshoes, but Natasha was finding it impossible to keep up. She was struggling far behind and they had to wait for her to catch up.

They had gone scarcely a mile when Fargo heard above them the sounds of pursuit and he knew that the count and his men had reached the gap and were coming after them. Natasha, struggling down a steep slope, tumbled and fell. Fargo helped her out of the deep snow.

"I'm holding you up!" Natasha said, tears of frustration streaming down her face. "Please, leave me behind. Save yourselves."

"Take off the snowshoes," he said to Natasha brusquely. Wordlessly, she complied.

Fargo stripped off her backpack and buried it hastily in the snow. He handed his to Dmitry and told her to climb on his back. She was light, but moving down the hillside on snowshoes while balancing her on his back was not going to be easy. They started off again and made better time.

"Just relax," he told her. "Like a sack of flour."

He heard the voices of the men behind them grow fainter and fainter as the morning wore on. Still the snow continued to fall and he was thankful for it. Without the wind and snow, their tracks would be so easy to follow that they wouldn't have had a chance of getting away.

All that long afternoon as his body fought the snow, the cold, the distances of miles and miles of running, he thought again and again of the image of White-Walker dropping dead on the snow, shot by Bull Slade, and the rage ran in him, only partly assuaged by the memory of the hole he'd put through Slade's shoulder. He thought of White-Walker's father, Fish-Seer, and of the old man's prophecy of death. Maybe Fish-Seer had seen the death of his own son and that is why he would not say what it was. But maybe the old man had seen that they would all die and did not want to tell them. And he wondered what was happening back at base camp. He hoped Sixty and Water-Song had been safe. Most of all he wondered how the count and his men had managed to track him and White-Walker all the way to the hideout.

By nightfall, Fargo was exhausted, but they

kept going in the darkness, ignoring the cold and their weary muscles. Dmitry was uncomplaining but he was tired and limping. They had descended from the high country into the low hills, passing quickly through territory that he and White-Walker had taken several days to search. The base camp lay below in the big valley. Fargo led the way around the marsh and across several hills to a point on a hilltop where he could see down behind the big rock where the camp was secreted.

The fires were lit and there were some men on guard—maybe four or so. The dogs had already dug in for the night. Fargo left Dmitry and Natasha in a snowy thicket on the hillside and quietly stole toward the camp for a closer look. And he'd try to get Sixty and Water-Song away from the camp before the others returned.

In an hour he had crept close enough to the camp to hear the words of the men. He pressed himself against the trunk of a pine, sheltered by its low limbs from the golden flickering of the campfire. Sixty and Water-Song were nowhere to be seen. He had barely got into position when he heard the barking of dogs in the distance. Fargo heard the sound more clearly. Approaching dog teams. The dogs in camp burst out of their snowbanks, barking and howling. Fargo hoped they wouldn't pick up his scent or if they did would recognize it and ignore him.

In another moment, a line of sleds pulled into camp and Victoroff, Slade, and the other men piled out. Fargo hadn't seen sled tracks and realized they must have found some alternate route up to the hideout and have hidden the sleds and the dogs there.

"You get 'em?" one of the men shouted.

"Shut up," Bull Slade shot back. He was holding on to his shoulder and his left arm hung limp.

"You say you are good fighter," Victoroff snapped at Slade. "And we get one man and that Indian. That is all. The rest of those criminals escaped! With that little bitch! You idiot!" Victoroff drew his hand to hit Bull Slade, then hesitated. Slade's face was full of hate and, Fargo noted, Victoroff had dropped all pretense of calling Natasha his daughter.

"Yeah, well I ain't finished yet," Slade said. "We'll get 'em. They ain't got supplies and they're on foot. First thing in the morning, I'll get that dog out again. It worked to find that hideout. And hell, it'll work again. Make that wolf dog hungry enough, and it'll act just like a bloodhound."

Just then, Fargo saw a dog tied to the back of one of the sleds. It was Long-Tooth and even though Fargo had seen it only four days before, he hardly recognized the wolf dog. It had been badly beaten and its coat was matted with dried blood. Its yellow eyes were wilder than before and it seemed to watch Bull Slade with a quiet unrelenting stare. So that explained how they had found the hideout. Bull Slade had used the sled dog to track them.

Suddenly Long-Tooth sniffed the air and looked around. His tail beat on the snow for a moment and he seemed to be looking right toward where

Fargo was hidden. Maybe the dog had caught his scent.

"So, how's our prisoners?" the count asked. "Got 'em safe?"

One of the men hung his head.

"She got away," he said, kicking the snow. "Hell, we was planning on having a little fun with her that night. Then she up and went."

"What?" the count roared. "What? Slade, your men are fools. Fools! And what about the old man?"

"Oh, we got him all right," the man said.

Fargo felt the shock run through him. Sixty? Dead?

"Found him out in the woods. Guess he was planning to get away. Found all kinds of stolen stuff out there—food and gear. Guess he'd been planning to run for a couple of days. Got him in the head."

Fargo remembered Sixty had said he'd put a cache out in the woods in case they ran into trouble. Well, he'd run into trouble all right. His last trouble.

"Just as well," Slade said. "Save us the trouble of killing 'em both later."

Fargo listened for a while longer but learned nothing more. He retreated quietly through the trees, his thoughts whirling. Sixty dead. White-Walker dead. And Water-Song run off, probably without supplies too. She didn't have a chance in a hundred of surviving. And in the morning, Bull Slade would be moving through the woods with Long-Tooth sniffing them out. How the hell could they outrun the sleds?

He felt the weariness and the cold assail him. More than anything, he wanted to turn back toward the campfire and just give up, lie down where it was warm. He pushed the thought away realizing that if he felt that, Natasha and Dmitry were certain to be in worse shape.

They were huddled where he'd found them, Natasha crying silently and Dmitry grim.

"She cannot feel her toes and fingers," he said. "I am afraid."

"We're going to die," Natasha said softly. "I know this."

Fargo pulled her roughly to her feet.

"Shut up," he said. "No more talk of dying. We're getting out of this. Now, it's a day's walk down to the river. And from there we can make the trading post. We can't light a fire. So, we're going to walk it. Night and day. Come on."

Hell, even if they kept going, Fargo realized, it would just be a matter of hours before the count and his sleds and dogs caught up with them. But moving on was better than sitting there to die. Or giving up.

"Fargo, I . . . can't," she said.

"You will," he said, bending to strap on her snowshoes.

They trudged on, leaving behind the big valley and descending through the darkness of the deserted valleys that led toward the mighty Yukon below. Morning dawned clear and cold. Fargo was carrying Natasha again, his back aching with the strain. Spots of light danced before his eyes as the exhaustion welled up. She was only half conscious now, moaning from time to time. Several times during the long night, he had taken her down and he and Dmitry had gently massaged her hands and feet until she cried out in pain as the blood circulated through the frozen flesh again. If they came out of this alive, he realized, she might lose a couple of toes. Her feet seemed to be the worst. But still, it was better than rape and death at the hands of Count Victoroff.

By afternoon, he heard them far off in the hills behind him. The barking of dogs echoed as the count and Bull Slade and his men came in pursuit. The distant sounds seemed to drive them forward faster. Natasha came to and clutched her arms around his neck in fear until he had to loosen them. Fargo pushed on, his legs leaden and aching with the effort of lifting the snowshoes against the heavy powder, his voice hoarse from exhorting Dmitry to keep going. The Russian's eyes were as blank as death, his face ashen with tiredness, and several times Fargo had to pull him along physically until finally he just kept going doggedly.

Just as the light was beginning to fail, Fargo paused at the edge of a pile of snow-covered rocks. Dmitry sat down wordlessly and hung his head. He let Natasha down and she sat whimpering and holding herself, rocking back and forth. They were in terrible shape, he realized. They couldn't keep it up for another night and Nulato, the trading post, was still a good ten miles off. The wind was bitter and night was coming. The snow had stopped falling and the white clouds had lifted.

Fargo looked across the hills below them and through the gaps he glimpsed the flat snowy plain of the frozen Yukon. For a moment, he thought he saw dark shapes moving below but when he rubbed his tired eyes and looked again, he saw nothing. His eyes, strained and nearly snow-blind, were playing tricks on him, he decided.

Behind them, the sounds of pursuit came nearer. Slade hadn't even needed to use Long-Tooth to track them, Fargo realized, because they had been too tired to even try to disguise their trail, and without the snowfall, the tracks were all too visible. Fargo turned his head and listened. They were only a mile away now. The end had come, he realized. And there was nothing he could do now except take a stand. The best he could hope for was to take out Slade and maybe even the count before they were overpowered.

"We'll turn and fight," Fargo said to Dmitry. The man lifted his head and a faint light flickered in his eyes. It seemed to warm Fargo and he felt the stirring of his own strength deep inside, a kind of well of fury that held all the heat left in his body, all the energy left in his life. If this was going to be it, damn it, he was going to go out with his guns blazing.

Fargo pulled Natasha to her feet and drove her to climb up to the top of the outcropping, a dozen or so feet above the trail. When they got to the top, Fargo's hopes rose. A small circle of rocks surrounded a flat area like a crown. Perfect for defense. The three of them crowded inside and removed their packs. Fargo pulled out the supplies and lined up the ammunition on top of one of the packs.

"You know how to reload?" he asked Natasha.

She nodded, pulled off her gloves, and took up one of the rifles and fumbled at it. She bit her lip and the tears welled up in her eyes as she looked down at her white fingers. She couldn't manage, Fargo saw, because of the frostbite. And she was scared. Hell, so was he.

"Never mind," he said gently. "You just hand us the ammo."

He and Dmitry fell to loading the three rifles. Between the two of them they could probably keep up a pretty steady fusillade, unless the men rushed them. Just as they finished, the sleds came into view. For a moment, Fargo hoped that they would just continue past, but Bull Slade, kneeling in the front sled, noticed the tracks by the rock outcropping and called a halt.

Fargo steadied the barrel of the rifle between two rocks, took aim, and pulled the trigger. The shot exploded and caught Bull Slade right in the arm, the same place he'd shot him the day before. Fargo cursed his bad luck. Slade shrieked and threw himself out of the sled and pandemonium ensued with men running every which way for cover. There was a line of rocks just to the other side of the trail and most of the men hunkered down there. Others drove the sleds off beyond firing range. Fargo looked for the count and finally spotted him in one of the rear sleds, but couldn't get a clear shot. Bull Slade was hiding behind a rock at the foot of the outcropping.

"Give up, Fargo," Slade said. "We got you surrounded now."

"Not without a good fight," Fargo shouted back.

A bullet zinged by his head from the direction of the line of rocks across the trail. Fargo could see some of the men scaling the opposite hill between the trees. Then he realized if they got high enough, he'd be exposed to fire. They wouldn't hold out as long as he'd hoped, he realized.

"It's hopeless," the count called. "Look, we make deal. Give me the girl and whatever criminals and you go free."

Fargo popped up and fired a shot at a man he spotted cowering behind one of the rocks on the hill. The man yelped and then fell to the ground. It was getting dark, harder and harder to see.

"Let's just camp here," the count called out to Slade. "Keep this rock covered. They can't last forever."

"No!" Slade called out. "I'm stuck down here by this rock. I want them shot now. Fire! Fire! Give 'em everything you got!"

Fargo popped up again and saw his opportunity. Slade had half stood, waving his men toward the rock outcropping. Fargo drew up his rifle and plugged him, once, twice in the head. Bull Slade's skull exploded and his body sank out of sight. As the bullets poured in, Fargo threw himself down on top of Natasha. The bullets rained in on them, ricocheting off the rocks with ear-splitting whines. Dmitry jerked and cried out.

"Get ya?" Fargo shouted to him.

"Only in the leg," Dmitry moaned.

There was no use trying to return the fire, Fargo realized, because there were so many bullets flying around them. They would just have to keep low until it lightened up.

The firing redoubled, the men shouting in fury and anger. As he lay on top of Natasha, Fargo felt a kind of dreamlike relaxation come over him and he fought it, knowing it was the exhaustion and the cold, it was his body giving up and his mind becoming cloudy. It was the first time he had lain down in two days. But as much as he struggled against it, it wrapped him in a kind of warm blanket and the gunfire seemed to be coming from very far away, so many bullets and the screaming of men, dying screams. Suddenly, he realized that the bullets were not whining around him. The bullets were no longer ricocheting through the rocks of their hideout and yet the firing was continuing. Men were shouting and screaming. There was a battle going on.

Fargo gritted his teeth and roused himself, pulling himself up slowly toward the top of the rocks and peering over them. Men lay all around the outcropping, their bodies dark on the dusk blue snow. Not far off, other men were grouped behind a sled, firing upward into the woods and the shouts and screams echoed through the trees. And someone was climbing up the rock outcropping. A big man. For a moment, Fargo blinked his bleary eyes and thought it was Bull Slade, come back to life.

"Rachlevsky!" the big man called out. "And, Fargo! Are you here!" Then the big man spoke in

Russian and Fargo suddenly recognized Maxim, the trader from Nulato.

"Hey!" Maxim said, clambering into the rock circle. "You alive here? Indian girl she come tell us you in trouble. We come. Time for Russians stick together against bad boyars."

Fargo grasped the big man's hand gratefully.

"Water-Song? She's all right?"

"She strong woman," Maxim said. "Wanted to come to big battle. I say, no. Hard trip. Stay here and rest. We Russians go." He jerked his thumb over his shoulder. "Lots of traders angry at Victoroff. Many know him from Ukraine. Always he cheats anybody he can. So we come."

Behind him, Fargo heard Natasha stirring. He pulled her up to her feet and saw Maxim's eyes get large. Maxim bowed to her and she collapsed against him.

"Got a bad case of frostbite," Fargo said.

"She is beautiful," Maxim said in awe. "I take care of frostbite."

He spoke to her in Russian and she smiled up at him and nodded. Dmitry struggled to his feet and took a faltering step. His leg was shot bad. Fargo put on a tourniquet, which Dmitry held tight.

The sounds of the battle were dying down. Bull Slade's men had either been killed or had run off into the woods. Fargo and Dmitry climbed down from the outcropping. Maxim followed, helping Natasha, with awe written on his face. Fargo smiled to himself. The two seemed made for each other. He could well imagine Natasha taking charge of the trading post and Maxim being happy to have found his Russian woman at last.

The sounds of shouting drew their attention. The Russian trappers had built a huge bonfire over by the trees and someone had lit it. The flames leapt upward. By the light of the fire, Fargo saw the group of men throwing a rope over a branch of one of the trees. As he watched, they put a noose around Count Victoroff's neck. The aristocrat was struggling, trying to break free, cursing them in Russian.

Then with a mighty heave and a shout, they hoisted him up into the air and he kicked his feet in agony. It took a long time for Count Victoroff to die. And Fargo, thinking of Pete MacKenzie, of White-Walker, and of Sixty-Mile Sam, watched every minute of it.

LOOKING FORWARD!
The following is the opening
section from the next novel in the exciting
Trailsman series from Signet:

**THE TRAILSMAN #164
NEZ PERCE NIGHTMARE**

*1859, The northern Rockies—
where a powder keg of bloodshed
was set to explode . . .*

Men who were careless by nature seldom lasted
long in the rugged Rocky Mountains. One of the
first lessons Skye Fargo had learned about living
in the wilderness was to always keep his eyes
open, his ears alert. The slightest of movements,
the faintest of sounds, might be all the warning he
had of an enemy's approach.

So this day, as the Trailsman wound down a
pine-covered switchback toward a series of rolling
foothills, he reined up on seeing a pair of large
ravens take sudden wing from the top of the nearest hill. Ordinarily when ravens took flight it was

hardly cause for concern. But this pair squawked loudly, as ravens did when upset by something or other. He waited to learn the cause.

Moments later a number of riders swept over the crest of the hill and headed in Fargo's general direction. In the lead was an Indian who rode with reckless abandon, as if his life were in danger. And perhaps that was the case, since the five men after him were all white and all had rifles in their hands.

Skye Fargo stayed hidden among the pines. Another lesson he had learned was not to meddle in the affairs of others. Whatever this involved was none of his business. For all he knew, the warrior had been part of a war party that attacked the whites, or perhaps the brave had been out on his own, looking to count coup. Fargo was in no position to make judgments.

Then, at the bottom of the slope, the Indian's Appaloosa stumbled in a rut and crashed to the ground, throwing the rider a dozen feet. Dazed, the warrior tried to rise and flee but his pursuers were on him in a flash. A burly man leaped from a sorrel, tackled the Indian, and pinned him while the others reined up and dismounted.

Fargo saw the warrior hauled erect and held while one of the whites bound his wrists. Once the Indian was helpless, his captors started cuffing him and shoving him around. Twice the warrior fell and was kicked so viciously it was a wonder he could stand again afterward.

The burly rider, who appeared to be the leader,

produced a rope. Laughing and joking, the five whites led the Indian to the nearest tree. The rope was tossed over a low, straight limb. Apparently the warrior had no idea what they had in mind because he let them position him under the branch. Once they tried to slip the noose around his neck, however, he struggled fiercely.

Fargo had seen enough. Hanging was a terrible way to die, a fitting end for cold-blooded murderers and horse thieves and such, but not for an Indian whose only crime was doing that which came naturally. He deliberately rose into the open and trotted down the switchback to the valley floor. One of the whites spotted him and at the man's yell all of them turned.

Fargo had a knack for reading people as well as he read tracks. As he drew nearer, he studied the faces of the five and did not like what he saw. These were hard, cruel men, all dressed in buckskins similar to his own. They had shifty eyes and the sort of wary looks that came from guilty natures. In short, they were up to no good.

Their prisoner was another story entirely. Up close, Fargo discovered the warrior was no more than a boy, a stripling hardly old enough to be allowed to go on a raid. By the youth's style of dress and hair, Fargo identified him as a Nez Perce. That in itself was mighty peculiar, since the Nez Perce tribe had always been friendly to whites. In fact, they were about the friendliest Indians who ever lived. Why then, Fargo wondered, were these men set to hang this one?

The burly leader, a rifle held at waist level, regarded Fargo with annoyance. "You want something, mister?" he demanded.

Fargo drew rein and looped them around his saddle horn to free both hands. He plastered a fake smile of greeting on his face and said, "Just thought I'd watch the hanging, or is this a private string party?"

"It's private," said the burly one.

"Ride on," added a skinny man wearing a beaver hat.

Fargo ignored both of them. Nodding at the youth, he asked casually, "What did he do to deserve to be guest of honor at a necktie social?"

"Not that it's any of your business, mister," the burly one said, "but the little red bastard tried to rob us. Snuck right into our camp and was making off with one of our guns when we saw him and gave chase."

"Strange," Fargo said.

"What is?" snapped Beaver Hat.

"He wasn't carrying a gun when you caught him." Fargo gestured over a shoulder at the switchback. "I watched the whole thing from up there."

The burly spokesman glowered. "Maybe he dropped it while we were chasing him. You ever think of that?"

Just then the young brave surprised everyone by speaking up in clipped English. "That not true!" he cried. "I not take gun. I not take anything."

Beaver Hat took a step and slapped the Nez Perce across the mouth with such force both of the boy's lips split and blood poured down his chin. "Shut your mouth, you mangy cur! You're going to die, and that's that." He glanced at the spokesman. "What the hell are we doing talking to this busybody Grant, when we have a job to do? Let's get it over with so I can get back to that sweet filly of mine at Fort Benton."

Grant hefted his rifle, then cocked an eye at Fargo. "You heard Brice, mister. We don't need to explain ourselves to you. Mind your own business and move on or you're liable to find yourself in more trouble than you can handle."

Fargo gave each of them a look in turn, meanwhile lowering his right hand until it hung within inches of his Colt. "I doubt the five of you could handle a bear cub, much less someone old enough to shave."

For all of five seconds the five hardcases stared in mixed disbelief and anger. It was Brice who had the shortest fuse, as Fargo knew he would. The man in the beaver hat whipped his rifle up, his thumb curling around the hammer, his features etched with resentment. Here was a born killer, a man who would gun down another at the drop of an insult. Only this time he picked the wrong person to try and gun down.

Skye Fargo's right hand was a blur as he swept

the Colt up and out. He stroked the trigger once and the revolver belched lead and smoke.

Brice, cored through the forehead in the act of squeezing off a shot of his own, stiffened and staggered rearward, his rifle banging into the ground. He did a swift pirouette to the ground and lay still, the rifle still clutched in his limp fingers.

The others had frozen in the act of bringing their own weapons to bear. Fargo swung the Colt from right to left and back again, ready to fan off as many shots as were needed if the four who were left wanted to make an issue of it.

Grant set the tone for his companions by slowly lowering his gun and nervously licking his lips. "Now hold on, mister. There's no need to go around shooting folks. We were just fixing to scare you off, not hurt you."

Fargo kneed the stallion forward until he was alongside the burly cutthroat. "I don't like being lied to," he said, and kicked the liar flush on the mouth.

Sputtering and gurgling, Grant crumpled to his knees, the rifle falling at his side. He covered his mouth with his hands to staunch the flow of blood, then twisted to glare at Fargo and blubbered, "You had no right to do that!"

"Just as much right as you did to hang this boy," Fargo countered. He leaned forward and barked, "Lose the hardware. Pronto." Four rifles, seven pistols, and four glistening knives hit the ground. "Now untie the Nez Perce and take the noose off. And be quick about it or I might lose my temper."

It was amazing how fast they could move when properly inspired. The youth hurried to the Appaloosa, rubbing his wrists where the rope had chafed his skin. He paused when about to mount and addressed Grant. "This not over, white-eye. Tell him to let us alone. Tell him it is ours."

Grant sneered. "You'll have plenty of time to tell him yourself, boy. He'll want your hide worse than ever when he hears about this." Grant looked at Fargo. "And your hide too, stranger."

"A lot of people have tried to take it before," Fargo commented, taking his reins firmly in hand, "and I still have it." He stared at their horses, pondering how best to avoid further gunplay, and announced, "I want all of you to take your footwear off."

"Do what?" one of the others responded.

"Shuck the boots and moccasins," Fargo elaborated. "And be quick about it." To accent his point, he blasted a shot into the ground within an inch of the speaker's toes. While they obeyed, he told the brave, "Collect all their horses."

Presently four pairs of grimy footwear lay scattered on the grass. The hardcases shifted from foot to foot, two with toes poking through socks that had seen better days about the time of the Revolutionary War. "Damn," Fargo said, scrunching up his nose. "The smell would gag a skunk. It wouldn't hurt any of you gents to take a bath once a year or so."

"You're a funny man, mister," said a sinewy specimen who hadn't spoken yet. "Everyone knows that getting the body all wet is bad for the constitution."

Fargo sighed, then pointed at the crest of the hill. "Start walking. Don't stop until you're at the top."

Grant found his voice again. "You'd strand us afoot out in the middle of nowhere? Without horses and guns? Why, we won't last a week and you know it."

"I could last that long," Fargo said matter-of-factly. "But then it takes a certain know-how to live off the land. Maybe you boys should go back East where all a man has to do to eat is have the price of a hot meal." He paused. "I should leave you buck naked, like the Blackfeet did to John Colter once. But I doubt you have his grit. So once we're out of sight, you can come back down and fetch your guns. Your horses will be tied on that knoll yonder." Fargo indicated a low hillock to the south.

"We'll remember this, mister," Grant vowed. "One of these days we'll meet again, and then we'll see how high and mighty you act."

Fargo aimed at the man's head. "Shooting jackasses could get to be a habit with me if you don't stop flapping your gums and move your legs instead."

It was a sullen, spiteful quartet who turned and trudged uphill, picking their way with care to avoid prickly patches and sharp stones. All four glared back at Fargo now and again. If looks could kill, as the old saying went, he would be a dead man.

Someone else had the same thought. The young Nez Perce faced him and commented, "You make mistake, Iron Will. Those bad men. Very bad. You be smart to shoot them now. They try kill you, just like Grant say."

"They'll try," Fargo said, and studied the brave's smooth, frank face. He read honesty there, and character. "Why did you call me Iron Will?"

"That name I give you," the youth said. "You make men do as you want. You have will like iron." He touched his chest. "My name Small Badger. I be Nez Perce."

"I know," Fargo said. "Where did you learn the white man's tongue?"

"From missionary," Small Badger said proudly. "Study many moons. Work very hard."

"You've learned it well," Fargo complimented him, and suppressed a grin when the young warrior swelled like a bantam rooster. He checked on the hardcases and saw that they had covered less than twenty yards. "Faster!" he called out. "Unless you want to lean against a bullet going past." That did the trick. With Grant in the lead they scampered for higher ground.

"See?" Small Badger grinned. "Iron Will. Just like I say."

Fargo turned his pinto toward the knoll. The youth fell in beside him and scrutinized him from head to toe.

"Why you help me, Iron Will? Those be your people, so why you help Indian?"

"Do I need a reason to lend a hand when I see someone in trouble?" Fargo rejoined. "The color of a person's skin shouldn't matter when they need help."

Small Badger digested the comment in silence until they gained the top of the knoll. "You like my father, I think. He be great Nez Perce. Much courage make man very good."

"I wouldn't go that far," Fargo said, not caring to make more out of his intervention than was warranted. By this time the four hardcases were a third of the way up the hill, two of them limping badly. He felt an urge to go back and collect their guns, but didn't. Even bastards like those four needed the means to protect themselves, he reflected. Not far north of where they were lay Blackfoot country, and the Blackfeet were notorious for slaying any and all whites they found in their territory.

"What I do with horses?" Small Badger asked.

For an answer, Fargo climbed down and ground-hitched all five. Then he removed the saddles and saddle blankets and lugged them a few dozen yards off. "That should delay them a little longer in case they get the notion into their heads to follow us," Fargo mentioned as he forked leather again. "I doubt they'll bother, though."

"These bad men," Small Badger stressed. "You not know them like me."

"Why were they set to hang you?" Fargo inquired.

The young Nez Perce seemed about to answer, then his gaze drifted to the sun, which hung low in the western sky. "Maybe tell other day. Must go, Iron Will. Must tell father much blood be shed."

Fargo would have liked to question the youth about the matter, but raising puffs of dust the Nez Perce galloped westward, riding up the same switchback Fargo had descended just a short while ago. Presently Small Badger was lost among the ranks of emerald pines.

Grant and his companions were almost to the top of the squat hill. Fargo saw them staring at him so he grinned wide enough for them to see and touched his hat. Putting his heels to the sturdy stallion, he loped to the southeast, swung wide of the hill, and resumed his easterly course. His destination was Fort Benton, the sole outpost of civilization between the northern Rockies and the mighty Mississippi. After months in the harsh mountains he looked forward to relaxing a spell, to a friendly game of cards, a full bottle of whiskey, and a willing dove or two.

Twilight dappled the land with long shadows when Fargo decided to stop for the day. Since there was a chance he was being pursued, he chose a convenient gully as his campsite. He allowed himself the luxury of a small fire but did so under a tree so the limbs dispersed the smoke. Supper consisted of jerky and pemmican he had picked up from a band of Kalispels he met near Flathead Lake.

That night Fargo lay with his head propped on his hands, admiring the myriad of stars and listening to wolves howl, coyotes yip, grizzlies cough, and mountain lions scream. It was a bestial chorus that most newcomers to the wild found disturbing. Not so Fargo, who had been lulled to sleep by such sounds more times than he could count.

Before daylight the Trailsman was up and in the saddle. An hour later he scanned his back trail from a low rise but saw no sign of Grant and the others. They had wisely decided to leave well enough alone, he supposed.

Later that day Fargo received a shock that had nothing to do with them. He had spied the rolling plains a few miles ahead and wound down into a broad valley that would bring him out onto the prairie when he heard the lowing of cattle. Puzzled, he reined up, questioning whether his ears had played a trick on him. There were no cattle in that neck of the country.

Seconds passed, and Fargo hard a distinct moo. Curious, he made for the source and shortly came on a small herd of steers and heifers grazing on the high, rich grass. He stood in the stirrups, searching for cowhands or evidence of a ranch. Neither were anywhere to be found. Not knowing what to make of it, he skirted the herd and pressed on.

Fargo hated to think that cattlemen were moving into the remote northern Rockies. Not that he had anything against cowmen, but each year more and more of the uncharted country he knew so well was being swallowed up by sodbusters, ranchers, and the like. At the rate things were going, it wouldn't be another fifty years before the land was overrun with fences and church steeples. The thought was enough to make him shudder.

It took two days of hard riding to come within sight of the Missouri River and his destination. Fort Benton was misnamed. It had no connection with the military. The American Fur Company had built the post as its link to the rich beaver lands lying to the west. Of late the beaver had about been trapped out, but the company kept the fort going as a trading concern with various tribes. There was a rumor that one day the government would lease it for use by federal troops but so far that hadn't happened.

Skye Fargo slowed as he neared the outskirts. He had been on the trail so long that he thought it best to make himself presentable for the ladies. He used his white hat to slap dust from his buckskins and leggings. His bandanna served to wipe his face and neck clean.

A circle of Flathead lodges stood to the northwest of the fort. Closer to the stockade were over a dozen buildings, most frame affairs barely substantial enough to withstand being blown over by strong gusts of wind. Over half would be described as "dens of iniquity" by Eastern newspapers. Among them roved grizzled mountain men, bearded trappers, company employees, Indians, and more.

There couldn't have been more than fifty people in sight, yet to Fargo, who hadn't been among his own kind in weeks and in a town of any size in over two months, it was a mass of humanity. He tilted his hat back on his head and rode up to a rickety hitch rail in front of an establishment that boasted HELLACIOUS DRINKIN' LIQUOR on a crudely painted sign.

Fargo cradled his big Sharps in the crook of an elbow and strolled in through the open door. After the sweet scent of the prairie grass and the pure air in the high country, the reek of sweat and alcohol and worse unsavory odors gave him pause. He breathed shallow and ambled to the bar, actually a long plank resting on a row of upturned barrels.

"Howdy, mister," said the barkeep, a sallow man whose pockmarked face gave him the appearance of having been half pecked to death by an irate chicken. "What will it be?"

"Some of that hellacious liquor you brag about," Fargo said, smiling. "Whiskey would do nicely."

The bartender chuckled and winked. "I have some rye that will go down so smooth, it'll curl your toes before you realize you've swallowed."

"Bring it on." Fargo dug in a pocket, produced a coin, and smacked it on the counter. "And don't stop until I say so."

At a few tables nearby men were playing poker. Others sat around, idly passing the time. Roving among the customers were four painted ladies.

One was as large as the heifers Fargo had seen. Another had a mustache thicker than his own. The third smiled a lot, which in itself was admirable, but in so doing she showed off the black gap where her four upper front teeth had been.

Fargo took stock of them while sipping the rye. He'd about made up his mind to try somewhere else when the fourth woman turned toward him and he felt his pulse quicken. This one was a genuine beauty, a blonde with a trim figure and a face as creamy smooth as milk straight from a cow's teat. Just looking at her was enough to make his loins twitch with hunger.

"Just get in, did you?" the bartender asked while wiping the plank with a cloth covered with dead flies.

"Yeah," Fargo answered, feasting on the sight of the lovely dove. "What's her name?"

"Jezebel," the man said, "and she don't come cheap. Twenty dollars will buy you half an hour. Longer if she likes you."

Fargo nearly choked on his drink. "Twenty? That's twice the going rate anywhere this side of the Divide."

"Maybe so," the bartender said smugly. "But Jezebel is twice the woman you're likely find most anywhere else, so it all balances out."

"And I suppose you get twice the usual share?" Fargo said.

The smug smile widened. "Nothing gets past you, does it?" He slung the filthy rag over a skinny shoulder and snickered. "A man has got to make a living, doesn't he?"

Fargo had looked forward to treating himself to the silken embrace of a willing lovely, but twenty dollars was practically all he had to his name at the moment. His thoughts must have shown because the barkeep leaned toward him and spoke quietly so no one else would overhear.

"You might try the second table on the right, there. That old geezer with the floppy hat is Burl Hassof. Contrary buzzard, he is. Struck a vein somewhere up in the mountains a few weeks ago. Must have brought back hundreds in small gold nuggets." The man paused. "He loves to play cards but he's the worst poker player who ever lived. Everyone who sits in with him winds up winning a little. You might get enough to afford Jezebel."

"Maybe I'll try a hand or two," Fargo said, and then thought of a question he should ask. "Say, before I forget. I'm looking for a couple of friends of mine. Maybe you know them."

"I might. Everyone stops by here sooner or later if only to ogle Jezebel. Who are they?"

"Their names are Grant and Brice."

"They've been in lots of time. Friends of yours, you say?"

"Yes," Fargo lied, thinking it would loosen the bartender's tongue a bit more. He needed to learn all he could about them.

The bar-dog lifted his head and gazed over Fargo's shoulder. "Then this is your lucky day, mister. Grant just walked in the front door."

Ⓞ SIGNET

MORE EXCITING ACTION
FROM THE TRAILSMAN SERIES

☐ **THE TRAILSMAN #161: ROGUE RIVER FEUD by Jon Sharpe.** When Skye Fargo arrived in Oregon's Rogue River Valley, he couldn't understand why every gun was against him until he came face to face with his own devilish double—the deadly Dunn. Fargo was up against a man who was more than his match when it came to murder. (182189—$3.99)

☐ **THE TRAILSMAN #162: REVENGE AT LOST CREEK by Jon Sharpe.** Skye Fargo had to watch his back with a pack of men who would do anything and kill anyone for wealth . . . he had to watch his step with women ready, eager and willing to get on his good side by getting in his arms . . . and he had to watch a nightmare plan of revenge coming true no matter how fast he moved and how straight he shot.

(182197—$3.99)

☐ **THE TRAILSMAN #163: YUKON MASSACRE by Jon Sharpe.** Skye Fargo was in the most god-forsaken wilderness in North America—Russian Alaska, where the only thing more savage than nature was man. Fargo had to lead a cutthroat crew on a hunt for a missing beauty named Natasha and the murderous men who held her captive. Now it was up to Fargo to find his way through the blizzard of lies to a secret that chilled him to the bone. (182200—$3.99)

☐ **THE TRAILSMAN #164: NEZ PERCE NIGHTMARE by Jon Sharpe.** Skye Fargo just can't say no when duty and desire call. That's why he finds himself dodging bullets from bushwhackers as he hunts a mysterious foe bent on building a Rocky Mountain empire with white corpses and redskin blood. (182219—$3.99)

*Prices slightly higher in Canada

Buy them at your local bookstore or use this convenient coupon for ordering.

PENGUIN USA
P.O. Box 999 — Dept. #17109
Bergenfield, New Jersey 07621

Please send me the books I have checked above.
I am enclosing $_____ (please add $2.00 to cover postage and handling). Send check or money order (no cash or C.O.D.'s) or charge by Mastercard or VISA (with a $15.00 minimum). Prices and numbers are subject to change without notice.

Card #_____ Exp. Date _____
Signature_____
Name_____
Address_____
City _____ State _____ Zip Code _____

For faster service when ordering by credit card call **1-800-253-6476**

Allow a minimum of 4-6 weeks for delivery. This offer is subject to change without notice.

Ⓓ SIGNET

THRILLING ADVENTURES FROM
THE TRAILSMAN

☐ **THE TRAILSMAN #157: GHOST RANCH MASSACRE by Jon Sharpe.** Skye Fargo figured he was heading into danger when he answered a call for help from his old pal Hank Griffin. Hank wasn't the kind to scare easy—but even so, the horror that Fargo ran into in the terror-haunted mountains of Arizona was hard to believe and even harder to battle. (181611—$3.99)

☐ **THE TRAILSMAN #158: TEXAS TERROR by Jon Sharpe.** Skye Fargo was hunting the two most vicious killers in the Lone Star state, and he'd have to draw fast and shoot faster to outgun those mad-dog murderers. But the Trailsman was caught with his gun belt off and his guard down in the dusty town of Ripclaw. (182154—$3.99)

☐ **THE TRAILSMAN #159: NORTH COUNTRY GUNS by Jon Sharpe.** When a call for help from an old friend draws Skye Fargo north to Canadian Saskatchewan, he finds himself facing a tribe of killer Crees, a pack of poachers who piled up corpses as high as pelts, and a mysterious mastermind carving out an empire of evil victim by victim. (182162—$3.99)

☐ **THE TRAILSMAN #160: THE TORNADO TRAIL by Jon Sharpe.** When Skye Fargo pledges to lead a beautiful widow's herd of cattle and her rag-tag crew along a twisting Oklahoma trail, he does not depend on the notorious drunk Quince Porterfield to enlist him in the hunt for a kidnapped Choctaw girl. Now all Fargo can hope for is that he doesn't leave them all twisting in the wind at the first wrong turn. (182170—$3.99)

*Prices slightly higher in Canada

Buy them at your local bookstore or use this convenient coupon for ordering.

PENGUIN USA
P.O. Box 999 — Dept. #17109
Bergenfield, New Jersey 07621

Please send me the books I have checked above.
I am enclosing $_____ (please add $2.00 to cover postage and handling). Send check or money order (no cash or C.O.D.'s) or charge by Mastercard or VISA (with a $15.00 minimum). Prices and numbers are subject to change without notice.

Card #_____ Exp. Date _____
Signature_____
Name_____
Address_____
City _____ State _____ Zip Code _____

For faster service when ordering by credit card call **1-800-253-6476**

Allow a minimum of 4-6 weeks for delivery. This offer is subject to change without notice.

⓪ SIGNET

JON SHARPE'S WILD WEST

☐ **THE TRAILSMAN #147: DEATH TRAILS.** Skye Fargo was riding into double-barreled danger when he hit the trail in Texas teeming with murderous Mescalero Apaches and brutal *banditos*. He was out to settle the score with a trio of bushwhackers who had bashed in his head and stolen his roll. The only thing that the Trailsman could trust was his trigger finger in a crossfire where lies flew as thick as bullets and treachery was the name of the game. (178823—$3.50)

☐ **THE TRAILSMAN #148: CALIFORNIA QUARRY.** Sky Fargo had gone as far west and as deep into trouble as he could get on San Francisco's Barbary Coast. Now he was heading back east with a cargo of dead animals, a dodo of a professor, a stowaway pickpocket, and a beautiful fallen dove fleeing her gilded cage. Hunting them was Barbary Coast bully boy Deke Johnson and his gang of killers.
(178831—$3.50)

☐ **THE TRAILSMAN #149: SPRINGFIELD SHARPSHOOTERS.** Skye Fargo could win most shoot-outs gun hands down—but this one was different. He was roped into a contest against the best in the West for a pile of cash that made the top gun worth its weight in gold. But when guns in the night started aiming at live targets, Fargo realized he had to do more than shoot to win, he had to shoot to kill ... (178858—$3.50)

☐ **THE TRAILSMAN #150: SAVAGE GUNS.** Skye Fargo is caught in a wild Wyoming war in which he must fight for his life in a crossfire of female fury, redskin rage, and the demented designs of a military madman who made war against the innocent and smeared his flag with bloody guilt. (178866—$3.50)

*Prices slightly higher in Canada

Buy them at your local bookstore or use this convenient coupon for ordering.

PENGUIN USA
P.O. Box 999 — Dept. #17109
Bergenfield, New Jersey 07621

Please send me the books I have checked above.
I am enclosing $_____ (please add $2.00 to cover postage and handling). Send check or money order (no cash or C.O.D.'s) or charge by Mastercard or VISA (with a $15.00 minimum). Prices and numbers are subject to change without notice.

Card #_____ Exp. Date _____
Signature_____
Name_____
Address_____
City _____ State _____ Zip Code _____

For faster service when ordering by credit card call **1-800-253-6476**

Allow a minimum of 4-6 weeks for delivery. This offer is subject to change without notice.

⊘ **SIGNET** (0451)

THE TRAILSMAN—
HAS GUN, WILL TRAVEL

☐ **THE TRAILSMAN #142: GOLDEN BULLETS by Jon Sharpe.** Skye Fargo goes on a Black Hills, South Dakota sleigh ride where he will have to do a lot of digging to uncover the truth about who killed who and why—and a lot of shooting to keep him from being buried with it. (177533—$3.50)

☐ **THE TRAILSMAN #143: DEATHBLOW TRAIL by Jon Sharpe.** Skye Fargo has a gunhand full of trouble when an Arizona gold vein gushes blood. (177541—$3.50)

☐ **THE TRAILSMAN #144: ABILENE AMBUSH by Jon Sharpe.** Skye Fargo was looking for rest and relaxation in Abilene, Kansas. What he found was five toothsome females who wanted to lead them over the plains in a couple of creaking wagons.... Skye said no, but the trouble was these lovely women wouldn't take no for an answer ... and they were willing to do anything short of telling the truth about the danger they were running from. (177568—$3.50)

☐ **THE TRAILSMAN #145: CHEYENNE CROSSFIRE by Jon Sharpe.** Skye Fargo ... in the tightest spot in his life ... playing his most dangerous role ... a man who everyone thought was a monstrous murderer ... with his life riding on his trigger finger and a woman's trust ... Skye Fargo fights a Wyoming frame-up with flaming fury and blazing firepower. (177576—$3.50)

☐ **THE TRAILSMAN #146: NEBRASKA NIGHTMARE by Jon Sharpe.** The settlers thought they had found a piece of paradise in the Nebraska Territory near the River Platte. But the trouble was ... a cougar named Nightmare, who killed without warning ... and a gang led by Rascomb.... What the farmers needed was a man who could kill a killer cat and outgun ... marauding murderers.... They got what they needed and more in Skye Fargo. (17876—$3.50)

Prices slightly higher in Canada

───

Buy them at your local bookstore or use this convenient coupon for ordering.

PENGUIN USA
P.O. Box 999 – Dept. #17109
Bergenfield, New Jersey 07621

Please send me the books I have checked above.
I am enclosing $_____ (please add $2.00 to cover postage and handling).
Send check or money order (no cash or C.O.D.'s) or charge by Mastercard or VISA (with a $15.00 minimum). Prices and numbers are subject to change without notice.

Card #_____ Exp. Date _____
Signature_____
Name_____
Address_____
City _____ State _____ Zip Code _____

For faster service when ordering by credit card call **1-800-253-6476**

Allow a minimum of 4-6 weeks for delivery. This offer is subject to change without notice.